1/24/2009

For Ola Kidd,

Enjoy the journey
and the End.

God bless,

Charolyne

# When He Calls

# When He Calls

## Sharel E. Gordon-Love

### La Caille Nous

Edited by Guichard Cadet

Cover Photo: Regine "Zekora" Romain
Cover Design: Shane Hudalla


Gordon-Love, Sharel E.,
    When He calls / Sharel E. Gordon-Love.
       p. cm.
    ISBN 0-9647635-9-1 (pbk. : alk. paper)
    1. African American teenage girls--Fiction. I. Title.
    PS3607.O595 W48 2002
    813'.6--dc21                                    2002024000



La Caille Nous Publishing Company, Inc.
PO Box 1004
Riverdale, MD 20738
www.lcnpub.com

Media & Distribution
328 Flatbush Avenue, Suite 240
Brooklyn, NY  11238
212-726-1293

For my Dad, Ronald A. Gordon.
Thank you for always being there for me.

# ACKNOWLEDGMENTS

First and *foremost*, I give thanks to my Lord and Savior, Jesus Christ for helping me to realize a life-long dream... I thank YOU!!!

To my parents, Ronald A. Gordon and Coretha Cobb, Mom and Dad to me!!! See? I didn't carry books around all the time for nothing. Something actually sunk in! ☺

To my children: Khayree (my eldest son), Alvin "Special" (my middle son), Ronald "Scooter" (my baby boy), and Sophia (my only daughter), the real loves of my life. Thanks for supporting your Mom! Oh, and I can't forget Maxx!

My SIBLINGS!!! Greg, Rhonda, Jeff, Mark and Danielle...and my nieces and nephew – Wafi, Janay, Tamara, Destiny, Takeya, Jada and Nyia.

Stephy D! Okay, Stephanie Hammett...my B.F. in Ohio! Yeah, yeah, I wanna give a shout out to my friend...LOL! So do I get a dressing room or what?

To my Pastor, Bishop Ivory W. Holden, thanks so much for your support! It means a lot to me.

To Pastor Kevin D. Ginyard, Sr., thank you for *always* telling me I can when I didn't believe I could. Your advice has been a great help in my life.

To some very special people in my life, Darlene Fraser...my big sister who has taught me many things I knew not, with the best sisterly advice and the biggest heart. I listen intently! Thank you for your prayers!

Freida Parker!!! My dear, *dear*... thanks for being there for me during a time I didn't think I could possibly make it through...and even now. Thank God for our 'hood...at Frankie's!

Tee Alexander...thank you for *understanding*. I appreciate that about you so much. Maybe one day soon? I hope so...most of all, thank you for making me LAUGH!

John Wilson–a very good friend! Who knew this would be the result of COGIC chat?

Finally, in memory of Christopher C. Gordon, my Granddaddy...I miss you terribly. Haven't met too many people who could beat you at playing the dozens!

For Grandma, Minnie M. Gordon, your advice is still priceless....and I am finally taking heed to it. You are always just a thought away...even in my dreams.

For my first big sister, my mentor and the young lady who led me to Christ, Patricia Faucette–a friend that sticks closer than any brother. I wish so many times I could pick up the phone and call you.

To Sylvia Lynn Stepney...my little sister with the booming voice that was stilled far too soon. Whenever I hear the song, "He Chose Me", I will remember what we shared and the part of you that is still with me–Sophia.

"...a most compelling novel. In its deeply profound simplicity, it reflects the spiritual insights of the Sharel I know."

*Bishop Ivory. W. Holden*
*Pastor of the Holy Tabernacle Church of God in Christ.*

"Ms. Love's gift for guiding her troubled and conflicted heroine through the challenges of her life is nothing short of marvelous."

*Pastor Kevin D. Ginyard, Sr.*
*Bridgeport, CT*

# Forsaken and Departing

*"Train up a child in the way he should go:*
*and when he is old, he will not depart from it."*
*Proverbs 22:6 KJV*

# Chapter One

It wasn't long before the ambulance came to take me to the local hospital. The blare of the sirens rang loudly in my ears, echoing with the pain in my head. After being beaten so severely, I could do nothing but lay still on the cold floor in an attempt to still the throbbing of my head as I tried to open my eyes and focus them. I could see people moving about, and I could hear them, but I couldn't tell who they were or what they were doing; just shadows darting here and there, some slow and some fast. It reminded me of a spook house I'd gone into as a child that required you to walk through. In the darkness I could hear sounds, but distorted and misdirected figures jumping out around which meant to confuse and scare me. My vision was poor and minimal at best, and the only thing I could to do was to feel my way. Exhausted from trying to make out my surroundings, I closed my eyes and allowed myself to drift into semi-consciousness. Then I heard two very loud footsteps head towards me with wheels turning and squeaking, the sound echoing through my head and all around me.

The attendants hurried inside the auditorium with their medical instruments, immediately examining my jaw, taking my pulse and shining a light in both of my eyes. They realized that I couldn't say anything when their questions were answered with moans of pain. I kept my eyes closed for the entire examination, the pain seeming to consume my whole body. My head throbbed, and I felt dizzy, as if I would fall if I tried to stand. My lips were so swollen I felt they covered my entire face.

My ears had a constant ringing that would fade in and out, never really going away.

I felt the gurney lifting me from the floor as the attendants carefully placed me on the stretcher, rushing me outside to a waiting ambulance. The ambulance sped off, sirens blaring almost before they closed the ambulance doors. One attendant continued to check for injuries and prepared an I.V. while the other communicated with the hospital giving them information about my condition and expected time of arrival. As I tried to force myself to wake fully, I could hear cars passing by with lightning speed. It didn't matter how fast they were going, I somehow felt that the passengers in those cars knew exactly what had happened to me. A strange feeling of paranoia and embarrassment fell over me, so I sought safety in the wooziness that began to take over my body. The minute I heard one of the attendants say we were nearing the hospital, I lost consciousness, no longer hearing or feeling a thing.

I awoke twenty minutes later to a light shining into both of my eyes again and an oxygen mask covering my nose. I had an overwhelming urge to vomit. The attending doctor tried to ask me questions, but by this time I refused to give a response, not even a moan. Since I couldn't cooperate, the nurses and residents turned my body from one side to the other, checking for more injuries, running fingers up and down my back, legs and arms. It wasn't until the doctor returned his attention to my jaw that I almost lost my mind; his touch sent searing pain all through me. I cried and moaned uncontrollably, kicking and thrashing about. I had never experienced that level of pain in my life!

Thirty minutes later, by the time my parents arrived at the hospital, I was on my way to ICU to be carefully watched for the next 24 hours. After I went through a CAT scan, x-rays and a few episodes of vomiting through my nose, the doctor decided to have me lie in bed in a semisitting position. I drifted off into a troubled sleep with the help of a shot of Demerol, bothered by my thoughts of the rehearsal that had gone bad and the events of the attack.

• • •

At first their voices sounded far away, but when my mother took my hand, I realized they were right there with me. Feeling the protection of my parents' presence, I opened my eyes and there was my mother looking down at me.

"Tonya, Baby, it's Mom. How do you feel?" she leaned closer to my face, taking my hand in hers.

I tried to answer, but I couldn't. All I could do was groan.

"I'm here, I'm right here," said Dad, hurrying to the other side of my bed, placing his hand gently on my shoulder. Looking into their faces, the pain they were feeling seemed to reflect mine, then I felt it over again as if it had not originally been. As usual they were trying to make it all better, only it was not better this time. It became very clear to me at this moment that their protection was only effective while they were with me, certainly not when I was alone. Realizing there was this lapse of protection sparked this anger in me, one I'd never felt with my parents before, almost to the point of me wishing them away. But as soon I saw my mother's tears and heard her soft sobs, my heart softened and I started crying too.

We cried together for a few minutes until the doctor knocked on the door and entered my room. He spoke with my parents in a hushed voice. Since I was not included in their conversation, I started looking around the room, noticing how small it was. I then had a sudden urge to get out of there. The monitor I was hooked to hummed and hissed, while the pressure cuff automatically took my blood pressure every 20 minutes. I'd almost convinced myself that I could tough out 24 hours until I heard the word surgery. The thought of surgery made me react violently. I tried to scream and attempted to get out of bed.

"It's all right, it's all right," Mom started saying, tears flowing non-stop as she held me in her arms to comfort me.

"Tonya, your jaw is broken. It...It's pretty bad. The doctor is going to try to reset it." Dad was trying to be strong for me, but I could tell he was fighting to keep the emotion out of his voice. I continued to protest, shaking my head 'no' and cried, my tears doing the pleading for my voice.

Even though I didn't want the surgery, it was set for the following morning at 6 a.m. Mom just held my hand and Dad continued to talk with the doctor, but this was not enough to console me at first. Easing onto the bed with me as close as she could get, my mother started talking softly in my ear, "Sweetie, you know your father and I love you very much...no matter what, we're going to be right here with you until everything is all right." She used to comfort me this way when I was around 5 or 6, whenever I thought there were monsters under my bed or in my closet. Mom would come and get in bed with me and tell me stories about David and Goliath, or a Bible story that sounded courageous and made me feel protected. Those stories and nothing my mother was saying could ease my current pain or erase a fear that I never knew could exist in the almost perfect life my parents created for me. When Dad joined us, sitting in the chair by my bed, the feeling of security I had when I was small flooded me. I remembered my bedtimes with my parents tucking me in as I eased into a peaceful sleep.

• • •

My parents have always been there for as long as I could remember. Kindergarten, runny noses and skinned knees; elementary school, bullies and school plays; junior high and my first cooking class; then high school, boys and dating. Ever since I could remember, everything in my life has been pretty much the same. I've lived in the same house all my life surrounded by the constant protection of my parents.

My father, Henry Henderson, Jr., is Chairman of the deacon board of our church and has been driving buses for the same company for fifteen years. My father, with his smooth dark skin, stands at six-one and weighs two-hundred fifty pounds, looking a little more threatening than he really is. Sometimes I think he should have been a preacher the way he can lay down the Bible to you. Almost make you feel like if you think wrong thoughts, you're going to lift your eyes up in hell and burn right then.

My mother, Delores Smith-Henderson, is an evangelist missionary, a stay-at-home mom, does a lot of volunteer work helping out at the church each week, or anywhere else she sees a need. Standing at about five feet, a little chubby with pecan tan skin and shoulder length hair that looks like it belongs on a baby's head. Her height could never begin to define the quiet strength she possesses. Her presence speaks volumes that even words couldn't come close to. Oh, she knows the Bible too, but she has a way of presenting it that lets you know when it's all said it done, you are the one to make the ultimate choice about your feelings concerning what she has shared. Mom is pretty in her own right. Her hazel eyes are something many a day I wished I'd inherited. I've often wondered how much competition my father had before they got married 'cause I have caught many men checking her out whenever we're out.

I can't say I've ever witnessed anything more serious than an argument between my parents. They had plenty of time to get to know each other well before marriage, having grown up and attended the same church we attend now. They started dating seriously when my father was a senior in high school, and married after she graduated high school the following year. I came along right after that, cutting their newlywed bliss short. They were young parents, but they both made sure my needs and wants were met. I was always under their watchful eyes.

Family time is important in the Henderson household, sharing our evenings at the dinner table, planning our yearly vacations and spending time with each other. My special place for vacation was the Poconos! That is where I learned horseback riding, and went on hikes and nature walks. I loved to sit between my parents watching TV at night before going to bed, laying my head on my mother's lap and putting my feet on my father's. There were times after I was tucked in bed unable to find sleep, I would sneak back down to see what grown ups did when little kids went to bed only to find my mother taking up my position in my father's lap, or catch them kissing. Tiptoeing quickly back up to my room, I would cover my head with my pillow so as not to laugh out loud after seeing that.

As much as family time is important to my parents, God and being in His service through the ministry of our church is just as important. My father oversees many projects in our church, particularly the finances coming in and going out, how and what it will be spent. My mother provided a supportive role to everyone, whether they belonged to our church or not, spending many hours down at the church giving out food and clothing, or lending a listening ear or a shoulder to cry on for a broken soul.

The church we attend, Christ's Redeemed Church of God in Christ, has gone through some extensive renovations to bring it up to date and to accommodate the many members we have now. There are close to 500 members the last time I heard, and the membership was still growing. The pastor purchased land on both sides of the church so that one side could be used to enlarge and extend the sanctuary to build better bathroom facilities, a few offices and classrooms, while the other side served to enlarge the parking lot. The basement was also renovated, allowing for a formal dining room, classrooms for children, and more bathroom facilities. The bricks on the outside were cleaned, and the frame was painted a fresh coat of white, while the grass was replanted and new shrubbery and plants were also planted to make the church look inviting. Once this was all done, our Pastor would have a fit when he saw anyone chewing gum, kids eating candy or attempting to write on anything that wasn't meant for writing.

Our current Pastor, Elder Richard Jackson, Jr. was not the original pastor of our church. His father, Elder Richard Jackson, Sr., is eighty years old and had pastored the church when my parents were growing up. After he became seriously ill about seven years ago, his son was placed in his stead and has carried on, making quite a few changes. The older folks didn't like it so much, but the rest of us did. The changes didn't take away from the fact that he loved the church, the people of God, and most importantly, God Himself. Proof of that is the time he takes with our church family, and what he is doing to better the church as a whole. He always seems to have time for you no matter what time it was, day or night.

Dad and Pastor Jackson act like they are brothers, and I guess they would since they have been friends since they were little boys. As they tell it, in their youth, they got into mischief together around the church, messing with girls and misbehaving many times during Sunday service. It's no wonder now that they are grown men my father has become the pastor's right hand man, helping him, literally, to run our church. Pastor

Jackson and his wife have three children, all who have gotten on my
nerves whenever our families would get together. They were all younger
than I am and all boys, playing in dirt, playing with worms and bugs, or
digging in their runny noses. What I couldn't understand was why I had
to play with them and be nice to them when they were always touching
me with their dirty hands. I would sneak in a hit or a pinch if they really
got on my nerves and just take the consequences of my actions once we
returned home. These were also times that my father and Pastor would
reminisce about growing up, wishing for the days of *yea* and *nay* to be
theirs once again.

## Chapter Two

After one week of nurses and thermometers, doctors and residents, blood pressure cuffs, and the occasional shot of Demerol or some other form of painkiller, it was time for me to go home. The only good thing about my hospital stay was my private room; one bed, a nightstand with a telephone, windows facing one of the parking lots, and a door that I kept closed at all times. I got up that morning and began collecting all of the get well cards that covered my nightstand, thinking the best thing to do was trash them since nothing they said had made me feel that I'd ever be well again. All week I feared this moment of going out in public with people staring and wondering, children staring, laughing and teasing. My face was still swollen from the beating and the surgery, my eyes puffy and achy, and my mouth wired shut so the healing process would go smoothly. To sum up how I was feeling, I felt really ugly!

The nurse assigned to me came in to help me to the bathroom to shower. She took me by the arm and led me to the door of the bathroom even though I no longer needed any assistance to take care of my personal needs. After I finished in the bathroom, I opened the door to the scent of the yellow tulips, red, yellow and pink roses, and the few plants I received, mingled with the antiseptic smells of the hospital. My parents had arrived, my mother picking up where I left off, collecting my personal belongings in a Lord & Taylor shopping bag to take home. My father was busy packing up the plants and flowers, putting them in a box he brought to carry them all. Ducking their hugs I retreated back to the bathroom to put on the clothes my mother brought for me to wear.

Before returning to the room, I felt compelled to take one last look in the mirror to see if anything had changed from the day before. My quick glance told me everything was the same; puffy red eyes, swollen and scab crusted top and bottom lips, black and blue bruises around my nose, and a bandage to cover the scar from surgery. Looking at myself in the mirror started an instant, throbbing headache at my temples, so I went back in my room to sit in the chair by the bed to wait for my release.

An hour before letting me go home, the doctor came in to examine me once more, giving my parents orders on how to care for my broken jaw. There was nothing serious for me to do other than sip everything through a straw since I was no longer weak from surgery and needing to receive nourishment through an I.V. There was no need for him to tell me not to try to talk since I couldn't and didn't want to. My father left my mother with the doctor while he gathered my belongings and gifts and took them to the car.

About ten minutes later an orderly came to my room with a wheelchair to take me down to the lobby of the hospital and to my father's car out front. Tapping my mother on her arm, I motioned a reminder for the scarf I requested the day before. I didn't want to go out in public with my face showing for the world to see. Reaching the double automatic doors of the lobby leading outside, I saw my father pull up to the door and get out, opening the two doors on the passenger side of the car for my mother and myself. My mother told the orderly that we were ready to go to the car, so he began pushing the wheelchair beyond the double doors. I closed my eyes and held my head down to avoid looking at other people or having them look at me though I had the scarf covering my face. After I sat down in the back seat of the car, I leaned down to ensure that I made no eye contact with anyone.

My father never drives faster than the state's speed limit of 55 mph, but just this once I wanted him to do at least sixty on the highway. My parents said no more than a few words between themselves the whole forty-five minute ride home. My mother would turn around every now and then to check on me, and I would pretend to be engrossed in reading the signs we passed. We were in the car together, but I felt as though we were living in separate worlds. My parents spoke softly to each other and held hands while I sat with my head turned to the window hoping neither of them would say anything to me.

As we approached our house, I untied the scarf and then retied it again to make sure the bandage was covered just in case any of our neighbors happened to be outside when I got out of the car. My father pulled the car up into the driveway as close to the back door as he could get it, and I made a quick dash to the backdoor and waited for my mother to open the door with her key. As I entered the kitchen, it felt like I had been away for months instead of seven days. I headed straight for the den, removing the scarf as I walked.

Our den has been designated the family room for as long as I can remember. The TV was in one corner, an old leather sofa on the side of one wall with a coffee table in front of it, and Dad's old leather La-Z Boy chair situated on the side of the room across from the TV. He usually took up his seat in his favorite chair to watch sports since my mother and I would stay away from the den during those times. There are several pictures of me when I was growing up, my parents' wedding picture, as well as pictures of my grandparents and other family members on the walls around the den. This was where I had told my mother I wanted to be during the day, so she had a pillow and blanket all prepared for me when we walked into the house. I could have gone to my room, but since my parents did not spend a lot of time in their room, I felt that I would be lonely upstairs by myself. By being in the den, I could hear what was going on and who came to our house.

The living room, my mother's fashion showpiece with custom fitted beige mini-blinds, carefully chosen black and beige sofa, loveseat and chair, matching area rug, end tables and lamps, was only used for special occasions. My parents used the living room when they conducted personal business or entertained special guests, but time with family and friends was spent mostly in the den. We ate dinner in the dining room unless there was something on TV we wanted to see. Those times we used trays and ate in the den. Other times my parents would take up their personal talks and discussions sitting around the kitchen table. This usually meant it wasn't for my ears. This is where my parents stayed the day I came home from the hospital. They discussed the situation and how they felt about it. Whenever I entered the kitchen, they stopped talking and my father got up to pour himself a cup of coffee or something. I would open the refrigerator, pretending that I wanted something, then close it a few seconds later, waiting for my parents to continue to talk. When they didn't I would leave the room and return to the den. The last thing I heard my father say was that he was still trying to make sense of it all.

Since my mother doesn't work, and my father works split shifts with the bus company, it gave him time to come home for at least three hours in the latter part of the morning. That gave them plenty of time to have various discussions or take care of business. The day after I got home, they were sitting around the kitchen table talking about what happened to me, sounding like they were not even talking about the same subject, but yet they were agreeing with one another. My father was saying that he just didn't understand how I could fall victim to such a vicious attack after the way I was brought up, and my mother would say something about believing in the power of prayer to counteract his negative words. I guess they were trying to make sense of it all. So was I.

For the next four or five days after my release from the hospital, our phone rang constantly, mainly members from the church calling to express their concern. They sent more flowers and more cards, making me feel like I was attending a funeral instead of recuperating. My friends Lisa and Sasha had sent me a beautiful plant and a card, and Denise sent me a card as well. Lisa and Sasha were still in school out in California and couldn't come to visit right away, but I couldn't understand why Denise had not come by since she was right up the street. Still I made it clear to my parents that I didn't want any visitors. There was no use in seeing anyone since I couldn't talk and I looked nothing like myself.

My parents intercepted my phone calls while they drank cups of coffee and discussed ways to help me deal with my recovery. They were talking about how they would convince me to allow people to come and visit me when the phone rang again, as it had been doing since I got home. Usually when my mother answered the phone, I tuned her out after she would say "hello" but when she said "How are you doing, Lisa?" I waited to hear more of the conversation.

"Were you able to keep your grades up? That's good!" my mother said, pausing and adding a few "uh huhs" and "that's right" as she talked to my friend Lisa trying to tell her without telling her too much about my attack, reassuring her that I was fine. Before she ended her conversation with Lisa, I had gotten up from my makeshift bed in the den and stood beside my mother listening, wishing it could be like it used to be. I would have taken my call in my room and told Lisa how things had been with me at school and inquired about any new guys in her life.

Lisa James has been my best friend since I was about five years old. She was the sibling I never had. We were like sisters, even falling out with each other on occasion, but never for any length of time. Lisa's family moved directly across the street from mine when I was two years old, although I only remember from the time that we played together at the playground before we started kindergarten. My mother made it a point to go over and welcome their family to the neighborhood and take me to play with Lisa. We didn't realize what being a friend was all about until we entered kindergarten together. The same playground that is in our neighborhood now was just being built. It only had swings and a sandbox back then. Our mothers would take us there at least two or three days out of the week so that they could talk and we could play. My mother and Lisa's mother became friends as well, but they were never best friends.

Lisa's family did not attend church, except Christmas, Easter or Mother's Day, but my mother and father would always invite them to come to our regular services. Lisa would come as often as she could when she didn't have to watch her brothers and sister, but as we reached our teens, she stopped coming altogether.

By the time we were ten years old, I realized Lisa considered me to be a very close friend. There'd be days that Lisa's family didn't have a lot to eat, so Lisa would make sure she was here at dinnertime. She told me that she never really went to bed hungry just unsatisfied because there wasn't always enough food at her house. Lisa started coming to dinner during the period that her father was laid off from work for several weeks. She asked me to make sure that this information remained *family business.* So I made sure I kept that information to myself, which resulted in gaining Lisa's trust and a closer friendship.

By junior high, we had become more like sisters, sharing our thoughts about boys, when we both got our monthly, and what we thought kissing and what sex was about. If you see Lisa, you would see me and vice versa because we did almost everything together. But keeping up with Lisa as we were entering our teens was a little hard since I thought about boys in a giggly sort of way, while Lisa thought of them in a sexual way. One day after school while we were sitting in the den at my house watching TV and eating snacks, she asked me if I had kissed a boy yet.

"Are you crazy? There is no way I'm going to kiss a boy until I'm old enough to date one. Besides, we have plenty of time to do stuff like that."

"Yeah, but if you ever did it, you'll like it. I kissed Darren under the stairwell after eighth period yesterday, and he liked it as much as I did," Lisa said as if it was no big deal, but that was the first time she had ever kissed a boy.

"Ooooo, no you didn't! I can't believe you!" I said while trying to imagine what it must have felt like.

I didn't understand why Lisa would even consider messing with boys like that when she had some serious things going on already. Her parents had given her the responsibility of taking care of her four brothers and sister while they were at work. She was the oldest, but she was only thirteen at the time! A few times, I suggested she should lock her brothers and sister all in their rooms and only let them out to eat. It sounded like a good idea to me, but Lisa would have gotten into big trouble with her parents because her brothers told every little thing.

Most days when we got out of school for the day, Lisa had to pick up her little sister from day care on the way home. Getting home would officially start her duties of making sure her brothers do their homework, heat up the dinner their mother had prepared before she left for work so they could all eat, and then make sure everyone had a bath and in bed by a certain hour. Her mother went to work from three in the afternoon to eleven at night. Her father didn't get home until around nine at night. I felt so sorry for Lisa, so I would ask my mother if I could go over and help out a few nights a week. Being there and seeing what Lisa had to deal with made me grateful that I was an only child because I couldn't imagine sharing my room or bed with anyone past a night or two. Baby-sitting with Lisa was always fun because we would play on the phone, making crank calls, or Lisa would call guys we knew in school and talk fresh to them while I listened and blushed.

The last week of eighth grade, my friendship with Lisa was put to the ultimate test. Lisa was fourteen and decided that kissing a boy under the stairwell was old junior high stuff, and she wanted to do some *high school type* stuff, like experience feeling a boy inside of her. The way Lisa put it was, "I'mma try this out to see what it's about, ok?" I would never tell her to her face, but I thought Lisa was stupid because she acted as if it was nothing to have sex with a boy. But with her mind made up, Lisa made plans to go away with her boyfriend for a whole weekend like they were grown or something. The guy was sixteen and in high school. Since Lisa's parents did not know him and had no idea that she had a boyfriend, it wasn't hard for her to come up with a plan and use me as a cover.

All I had to do was play dumb and say I knew nothing about Lisa's plans, but our parents could not believe I didn't know where she was. Lisa hadn't called home and after twenty-four hours, her parents put out a missing person's report on her. Coming home after her two-day rendezvous, Lisa strolled into the house with the craziest lie she had thought of to date... she told her parents that she took the train to visit her grandmother in North Carolina. The reason she didn't call home was because she got lost and just decided to come back instead of trying to continue on the train down south.

I could hardly wait to meet up with Lisa. Since we only had one class together, I had to wait until we were walking home from school, to hear the details. My mother had already told me Lisa was on punishment, but I wanted to hear about what happened with Lisa's boyfriend. Meeting by the front door like we did every day, I couldn't wait for Lisa to tell her story. We walked a whole block before I dared ask Lisa anything about her weekend. She had already pulled a tissue out of the side of her backpack to remove the mocha colored lipstick she put on in school every morning. Then Lisa pulled the knot loose she had tied in the front of her blouse to show her belly and fixed it properly inside of her jeans. I was always amazed at the things Lisa would sneak to do and then go through so much to cover up before she got near our block. By the time we turned the corner onto the long street that led to our own block, I couldn't stay silent any longer.

"I've been waiting all day to hear the details. From what your mother was telling my mother, you won't see outside until you're twenty-one." I was excited yet trying not to laugh.

"Do you really think I care? Anyway, do you want to hear about my weekend or not?" Lisa asked, flipping her book bag over her shoulder.

"Yes, and don't leave nothing out."

"First of all, it hurts real bad! It felt like he was about to break me in two. I was screaming all loud in the hotel and he kept putting his hand over my mouth so people wouldn't think he was killing me. It sure felt like he was. On top of that, I thought I got my monthly right in the middle of it, but come to find out, this is what happens when you lose your virginity," Lisa explained as if this was something as simple as picking out a dress.

"Do you think you will do it again?" I wanted to know, although I couldn't imagine how I would have handled myself in the same situation. Just thinking about a guy touching me in places that was considered private made me shudder with embarrassment.

Lisa didn't answer right away, but when she did, she said, "Yeah...I would. You know how something can hurt real bad, but then when you have time to think about it, you wouldn't mind doing it again? That's how having sex is. It's supposed to be easier the next time anyway, and it will feel good too, so yeah...I would do it again."

"Well did you at least..."

"Use a condom? Yep, I wasn't going to let him give me something I can't get rid of."

First loves, first hurts, Lisa and I have shared a lot of *firsts*. But that was the first time I covered a serious thing with a major lie to my own parents *and* someone else's, all the time fighting the urge to change my mind and just tell the truth. Lisa's weekend with her boyfriend changed the way she viewed guys, sex and relationships. It also changed the way I saw my friend; she was becoming a woman now and I was still a little teenager. Even with my mixed emotions about the choices Lisa had made about her sexuality, I realized that our friendship had grown to yet another level of trust.

• • •

The summer before we were to enter our freshman year of high school, and just a month after Lisa lost her virginity, we met and became good friends with two more girls.

Sasha had gone to the same school with us since elementary school and we knew her, to speak when we saw her, but I was in no hurry to become friends with her because she had such a smart and loud mouth. She was short and skinny and had the biggest mouth, always talking smack to all the other kids. We were all hanging out at the playground, as usual, when Sasha decided she would come over and talk to us. Lisa liked Sasha and became instant friends with her, so I figured I'd better go along with the program or risk losing my best friend. Sasha grew on me after a while, and I didn't mind her smart mouth too much unless it was directed towards me.

That same summer Denise moved to our neighborhood and it seemed that we were just meant to be friends. We saw Denise as she moved into her house with her brother and father because being nosy, Lisa, Sasha and I strolled down the street to see if any cute boys moved in. Instead of going over to introduce ourselves, we kept walking as if we didn't see her, while trying to get her brother's attention. Once we got down to the end of the block, we burst out laughing as if we really did something big. Her brother was cute, and we had plans to walk by as much as possible for the rest of the summer. Our excuse was that we had to pass by Denise's house to get to the playground.

We met and spoke to Denise for the first time down at the playground during a craft fair and dedication ceremony to unveil the new basketball courts and community center. My mother was on the church committee that put together the craft fair. The fair was also an opportunity for the people who lived in the neighborhood to get to know each other better. We had hot dogs, hamburgers, soda, chips, and cotton candy, just to name a few. Lisa, who is not shy, introduced herself, Sasha and me. She then fell into easy conversation with Denise.

"So where you from?" Lisa asked, taking a seat next to Denise on the bench where she was sitting.

"A suburb of Atlanta. I don't know if you ever heard of it, but it's called Smyrna."

"Why did y'all move here? I ain't trying to be nosy or nothing, but I didn't see your mother when you were moving in," Sasha said, snapping her gum in between her words.

Denise put her head down and said, "My mother didn't come with us."

"Oh..." Lisa and I said together. Then there was an uncomfortable silence until Lisa suggested we hit the food tables. We used that opportunity to change the subject. The four of us ended up hanging together for the rest of the day, exchanging phone numbers with Denise and planning what we would do for the summer.

That was the beginning of our foursome. Lisa, Sasha, Denise and I became inseparable, taking high school by storm while trying to get a grasp on life. Since we all came from different family backgrounds with trying experiences and times, I often felt that I was still a baby compared to them. Especially when it came to Lisa since she was no longer a virgin. She even talked like she had some newfound wisdom that I had yet to attain, and I was jealous even though I knew I wasn't ready for any of what Lisa was doing. After her experience with her boyfriend, Lisa didn't talk about doing it so much anymore, but she was always the one to give advice on the dos and the don'ts of sex and relationships.

Even with curfews, I was the baby. My curfew was always an hour earlier than my friends wanted to be out, and I could never squeeze an extra hour out of my parents. Their reasoning was that the longer I stayed out, the more chances that I would find trouble or it would find me. Sasha didn't have a real curfew. Denise could come and go as she pleased because she was home alone most of the time due to her fathers erratic work schedule. Her brother had just graduated high school, so he spent his time working at the local car wash and hanging out with his friends. According to Denise, he would be heading for boot camp in the Marines by the time we would be headed back to school.

Since we all attended the same high school, I would pick up Lisa then we would pick Denise up and then meet Sasha on the next corner to walk to school. Since we were all freshmen, we had the same lunch period and shared some of the same classes. After school, we met up in front of the school building to walk home together. This became our steady pattern each school day throughout the ninth grade. In our quest to *broaden our horizons* as Sasha put it, we started taking the bus to hang out at the local mall. Sleepovers were added to the mix and we each took turns sleeping at each other's house once a month. If walls could talk, the walls in our bedrooms would tell of all our deepest secrets. How we weren't interested in smoking cigarettes or getting high. How we felt about guys, our parents, school, religion, sex of every kind, what we read about it and if we planned to do it, and just what being grown was all about. We would laugh and talk for hours, instead of going to sleep.

$$\bullet \bullet \bullet$$

By the time we were sophomores in high school, our constant ritual was hanging out at the playground. That is where we caught up with all that was going on in our neighborhood, like who was going out with who, what girl our age or younger was having a baby, what guys were nice and who we considered to be *dogs*, Sasha's word of choice.

We turned sixteen and not much had changed in how I felt compared to my friends. As much as I pretended to possess the same maturity as they did, I would always get a dose of reality whenever my parents prevented me from doing the things my friends could. My friends could talk to guys and they could call them and even visit them, but my parents would not allow phone calls until I turned sixteen! The only boys I could talk to, without my father asking too many questions, had to be a member of my church, and I wasn't interested in any of them.

Just the fact that we were sixteen gave us a mutual feeling of thinking we were practically grown and knew quite a bit about the world and how it operated. We did since our world consisted of watching for cute boys and giving them our number, hanging down at the basketball court to be in direct view of them, and quite possibly talking to them on the phone at night. The occasional trip to the mall was the highlight of our existence, especially if we met some guys that didn't go to our school or live in our neighborhood. Our lives were truly that simple.

This summer was no different, in that we had every day to try to find something to do to keep us occupied but out of trouble. None of us wanted summer jobs because we felt that this summer would be totally different. As usual, Lisa was the exception. She worked at a daycare center three mornings a week while the rest of us slept in or found something else to do until she got off from work.

Our community offered summer camp, summer jobs, senior activities and organized sports to the residents who lived there, so it made no sense to try to find trouble to get into. We live in a small city in New Jersey, just forty-five minutes outside of New York. Our neighborhood was middle to upper working class. A lot of my friends who live on the west side of town have parents where the father works so the mother can stay home to look after the children. In other homes both parents work because for them it took two salaries to afford to live in our neighborhood.

There are a lot of benefits living on this side of town; a playground with nets on the basketball rims, working swings, clean sandboxes, sports equipment and someone to run the playground during working hours in the summer, and a community center that is open throughout the year. Our high school was just five years old at the time, and was one of the most technologically equipped in the state. Some people used a friend or a relative's address so that their children could get in and get the best education in this town.

Most houses have at least three bedrooms, one and a half baths, manicured lawns and hedges with sprinklers constantly going in the summer, new cars in most driveways, and well-dressed families. The community was quiet with hardly any burglaries or any other crimes on the west side, but you can pick up a paper and read about the east side's crime on a daily basis. The houses over there are mostly boarded up or run down, and they seemed to have a dirty odor all its own whenever I walked on that side of town. The only thing separating the west side from the east Side is the playground and a street block, but we did have something in common, and that thing was the mall.

Despite all the good things our community offered, there remained a certain level of temptation to do something we knew we shouldn't. I was too afraid to take a chance since I knew my parents and what they expected of me, but I would from time to time find myself entertaining thoughts of being with a guy sexually, or staying out after my curfew. The few times I had a chance to do it, Lisa told me to just say I was going to spend the night at her house so I could go to a party. When I weighed the situation and remembered my father's wrath, I quickly changed my mind. The restrictions on my life prevented me from ever carrying out these thoughts, so I thrived on the stories Lisa and Sasha would share.

Although nothing much had changed in my daily routine, turning sixteen changed a lot for me. At first I couldn't understand all the hype about this milestone age, especially since I still did the normal things, like always finding myself sitting on the sidelines down at the basketball courts. We found ourselves at the basketball courts almost every day that summer, and if it were not for the opportunity to talk to the guys when they took a break from playing ball, summer would have been dead.

That is until the day that James Barnett showed up.

The basketball courts were the height of attraction in the summer with guys coming from neighboring communities to play and brag about their skills. The overcast muggy day didn't keep anyone from crowding the sidelines to root for the team their friends played on. Every now and then a small child would stray away from their camp counselor. The courts didn't just bring the guys and my friends. Girls seemed to come out of the woodwork to hang out too, causing an occasional riff to break out over a guy.

My friends and I were just sitting there talking and watching the game when Sasha noticed there was a new guy playing. He was very aggressive on the court, snatching the ball and going to the hoop before his opponent could recover. You could tell the other guys didn't like him too much, but they seemed to have some kind of respect for him. I became very curious about him. He screamed *too cool* from all of his pores, with his crooked smile and slightly bowed legs, and a cool walk that he was either born with or had practiced many hours to perfect.

Without saying a word, Sasha got up and started walking towards the guys. They had just taken a break and were standing around throwing back sodas, so Sasha took that opportunity to introduce herself. They were standing in a group talking about their game when Sasha walked right up to the guy. As bad as I wanted to meet him, I would never be so bold as to go over to him myself.

It wasn't long before Sasha grabbed James by his left arm and headed over towards us to make introductions. James took over the conversation from there.

"What's up? How y'all doing?" James asked, flipping his baseball cap frontward and then backwards again while leaning most of his weight on his left leg. We all spoke and James was acting like he'd never seen a girl before the way he was staring at me all crazy. James finally said, "Tonya, that's your name, right?"

"Yeah," I said, feeling self-conscious under James' intense stare.

"You got a number? I might give you a call later." His stare never wavered as he smiled out of one side of his mouth.

"Yeah, but I don't have anything to write it on." I always carried a few pens in my backpack, but I knew Sasha went after him first and I didn't want her to think that I was trying to get with him. Plus, I didn't want to give him my number just like that. I had just met him. James insisted that I give him my number for him to commit to memory, so I did. He went back to playing ball with the guys, and I went back to watching him until Sasha came and stood in front of me.

"So what was all that?" Sasha wanted to know.

"What?" I feigned ignorance.

"Oh, so you're trying to act like you don't know. Anyway, it's all good 'cause it's too many other guys out here for me to talk to," Sasha said, taking a seat next to me. "But ain't he fine, girl?"

I just laughed because James sure was fine. It was like his presence demanded a respect that none of the other guys had. As I sat there trying to concentrate on what my friends were saying, my mind had already begun to concoct a romantic story between James and me. What it would be like to talk to him and get to know him, what it felt like to kiss him, to be in his arms. I never made it to sex because Lisa interrupted my thoughts.

"Tonya, where are you?" Lisa asked, waving her hand in front of my face.

"She's in 'James Land'," Denise said, shaking her head and smiling at me.

"Uh huh, she better get her head out the clouds 'cause he ain't on her like that. Besides, he wants somebody who's gonna let him know he's touching you in special places, uh, if you know what I mean," Sasha said, laughing while patting her neat hair cut in place.

"Whatever. I see he didn't ask for your number," was my weak response.

"How you know he didn't ask me over there when I was talking to him? Girl, don't you see him checking me out after he makes his shots? I thought you did!" Sasha said, hitting hands with Denise.

"Here *you* go," I said to Sasha as I continued to watch James fake out his opponent and make his next shot. He really was some kind of fine, and he smelled good too! I didn't know how he could still smell nice while sweat poured down the sides of his face, under his arms and down his back. I watched James handle the ball with ease, making the game of basketball seem like he invented it. He loudly kept his score so everyone would know he was winning, and he would celebrate after each basket he made by standing back with his hands still in motion of his shot and say, "Swish! Yeah, like that, just like that!"

So until we decided to leave the playground, I divided my attention between my friends and James, the new guy in the neighborhood who had game in more than just basketball.

• • •

The weeks after meeting James at the basketball court, we split our time between each of our houses, the mall and the courts. However, the courts became my favorite place to be since I was able to see and talk to James. He was the first guy I was really attracted to, and I found myself playing our conversations over in my mind each night as I lay in bed before drifting off to sleep. Some of the stuff that came out of James' mouth either had me laughing or thinking hard. Each day before I left to go home, James would ask me when I planned to invite him over to my house. I always came up with some lame excuse as to why he couldn't since I knew my father wasn't trying to hear a thing about guys coming to visit me. Convincing my father would take a miracle, so I figured what better way to get through to him than through my mother. I started on her the first day James asked to come over my house. I was hoping my mother would help me convince my father to allow me to date before the summer ended.

My mother told me she didn't mind James coming to visit and she promised to work on my father. Although my father agreed some time ago that I could start dating at sixteen, he pretended he couldn't remember any such thing. Just mentioning that a boy was interested in me caused some serious discussions to take place in my house. It still took weeks of pleading, begging, the use of creative thinking and anything else I could possibly come up with until I was able to convince my father that I could be trusted. I would say things like, "I'm no longer a little girl and that someday I will be getting married," or "You will like James because he's independent and he knows what he wants to do in life. You like people like that, Dad," to "Mom, please tell Dad that I'm ready for this…please?" I even started doing things around the house without having to be told to prove my point. So with my mother's

Sharel E. Gordon-Love

assurance, my father allowed me to have my first male visitor, on the condition that he knows where James lived, what he planned to do with his life, and a host of other things I couldn't vouch for.

The day my parents agreed to allow James to visit me, I ran to my room to phone him with an invitation to come that same evening. While waiting for James to arrive, I prepared a bowl of chips and glasses of soda for us. As I turned on the TV, I heard the doorbell ring. My heart started beating fast as I started for the door but my father, who was ahead of me, answered the door. James came in and took his cap off as I introduced him to my father. Shaking James' hand, my father welcomed him into our home just as my mother came from the kitchen wiping her hands on her apron. I introduced James to my mother and then we went to the den while my parents went to the kitchen. As soon as he entered the room, James shut the door behind him! Before I knew it, my father had it opened again, and I didn't have a chance to do anything or say anything in my defense. My heart was racing so fast, I felt like I had just run around the block ten times.

"Young man, I'm not going to have you visiting my daughter behind a closed door. Leave this door open." His tone let James know he wasn't even playing.

"Aw, yo, I'm sorry. Check it, we ain't even gonna be doing nothing," James said, using his street lingo as if not acknowledging my father as an adult.

"I know you're not going to do anything. Tonya, you know better," said my father, shaking an accusing finger at me.

"I was...um..." I said, knowing my father wasn't hearing a thing I had to say.

"Just make sure it doesn't happen again," said my father, squinting his left eye almost closed. I knew I was going to hear it real good when James left.

I was embarrassed and speechless when my father left the den headed for the kitchen. James moved closer to me and put his arm around me as if nothing really happened.

"What's up with your pops? He act like we was gonna take our clothes off or something," James said, sounding a little annoyed.

Removing James' arm from around me, I said, "My parents are old school, and my father just don't play when it comes to me, so..."

"So what? You invite me over and all of a sudden there's all these rules," James snapped, putting his cap back on his head. I just looked at him as if he was crazy.

Putting his arm around me again, James said, "Can't I at least touch you a little bit? That's why I came over here. Besides, I don't like to be all out in public showing affection to my girl."

"Didn't know I was your girl," I said, blushing. This time I didn't move James' arm, and tried to move a little closer to him.

"Trust me, I don't spend much time with someone if I wasn't planning to have something with them," James said nuzzling my neck causing me to pull away once again.

"Maybe I would know I was your girl if you asked me. All we ever do is talk down at the courts and on the phone."

"What you saying? You ain't my girl?" James asked, stopping his attempts to kiss my neck.

"Well, uh, like I said, you never asked me," I said, moving away to put more distance between us while trying to listen for my parents.

"Okay then, Tonya...this is so corny, but will you be my girl?"

"Let me think about it..."

31

Sharel E. Gordon-Love

"Oh so you got jokes," James said, removing his arm. "I ain't trying to force nothing, but you know, if I were you I wouldn't think about it too long."

"Okay then, we can go out, but I'm telling you right now, I am *not* into having sex. I have never and I don't plan to any time soon."

"Who said anything about that? I'm just trying to get something going between you and me. Come here, Girl," James said, surprising me with a kiss on my lips.

"What are you doing? I don't want my parents to catch us!" I said in a low voice.

"This is what happens with a guy and his girl, didn't you know that," James said, kissing me again. Wanting to kiss him and fighting to keep James from kissing me was more of an annoyance than anything else because I had to keep an ear out for my parents. He didn't seem too worried about the fact the door was open and my parents could walk in at any time.

James stayed for about two hours that night, but ended up complaining that we didn't have any real privacy to kiss and for him to feel me up. It wasn't like I had kissed a boy before; much less let him feel on me. So the comfort of being in the den with my parents not too far away was good for me. The thought of being alone with James caused some new feelings to course through my body, so I didn't need an opportunity to act on them.

That first night with James gave me a chance to really take in his physical body, and make an attempt to see just where his head was other than in that blue baseball cap. What I learned was that the Yankees are his favorite team, so he had to 'represent' by wearing the cap with their logo on it. Name brand clothes were a must, jeans sagging at just the right place on his slim, but muscular body, with a pair of blue and white Nikes to match the cap.

James was also all into himself! All he did was brag about how he and his boys scheme on the girls, and how the girls are ringing his phone off the hook. His beeper did vibrate the whole time, but he never bothered to check to see who was beeping him.

My response to all of this was pretending I was impressed all the time thinking to myself, "yeah right!" He was a handsome guy and all, but he ain't all that. In spite of the negatives, I still found myself fascinated with the person James was trying to convince me he was. Only because I believed I could really get to know him and find a sweet guy instead of the rugged, tough guy out to get his without any thought for anyone else. His handsome features and personality that insisted you pay him your utmost attention didn't hurt too much either, but it wasn't enough to make me give in to his advances.

Sure enough as soon as James left, my father started right in, reiterating the condition on which James' visit was based. He wanted to know where James was from, and made it clear that James had really gotten underneath his skin. Since I had never gone to James' house, I figured stating this fact would stop my father's line of questioning and remarks, but he continued. By the time my mother had her input, I was past trying to control my frustration, and it played out when I answered one of her questions. My mother made her point and chastised me almost all in the same paragraph ending it with, "…and that tone? You'd better take it down an octave or two."

"It's just something about that boy I can't put my finger on," my father started in again, scratching his head as if he were carefully thinking the words he was about to say. Nodding his head agreeing with his next sentence, he said, "He's just downright rude and disrespectful."

I tried my best to explain my friendship with James, but my father just went on and on about what he thought about James and any kind of friendship I called myself having with him. That is the point where I decided to tune my father out and hope that I put the 'yes, Dads' and the 'uh huhs' in the right places so he wouldn't realize I wasn't paying attention to what he was saying. It sounded like a bunch of gibberish to me, so I decided right then and there that it was time for me to start making my own decisions concerning James.

I didn't tune back in until my mother asked me if I had stacked the dinner dishes in the dishwasher. It was her way of making sure I did my chores. She helped me clear the dishes from the dining room table and proceeded to straighten the kitchen while I pretended to listen to my father complain about my disrespectful boyfriend. Mom said I'll understand what they're talking about when I have children of my own, but at that very moment, I wasn't feeling any of it.

In spite of my father's occasional opinions and remarks, James and I continued to see each other, becoming closer throughout the summer. Dating for us was meeting at the basketball courts to talk, and sitting in my den for a few hours a week. My father said James could come over every other day, but never on Sunday. He feared that if we spent too much time alone, we would kiss or something. By this time, kissing had already become a constant part of our friendship.

I found myself thinking about James when he wasn't around me, writing his name on the front of my journal with mine, drawing hearts next to both of our names. Whatever I decided to wear, I would always consider choosing something in blue, James' favorite color, or something that I felt he would like in order to hear his compliments. I even thought about him when I combed my hair, hoping he would notice when I changed my hairstyle. No wonder my parents didn't want me to date. My parents should have explained things to me a little better than to just say I don't need to be serious about one boy. Feelings of obligation came into play, making me feel like I owed it to James to talk to only him. He had the nerve to get a little angry when I would talk to a guy that I knew! What I couldn't stand most of all was that James expected me to be home when he called, or at the courts unless I told him I had other plans.

By the time summer ended and school was about to begin, James was acting like I was the finest girl around. As far as his true attraction to me, I really couldn't say. He claimed he loved my dark skin, my pretty hair and petite shape. My skin had always been clear and I never had any problems with pimples or anything, so that part is understandable. Having the kind of hair that needed only a damp brush and a little pomade, I was set, so I can get with that too. But my shape? If 32-24-34 was considered a shape on a five, two, one hundred twenty pound frame, I could even get with that. But by my own standards, I wouldn't have considered myself *pretty*. I had been told I was cute for as long as I could remember, so I could settle for that.

The night before the first day of school, James and I were sitting on the porch discussing our plans for the new school year. James planned on making the varsity basketball team, and I was going to concentrate on singing. That night he finally decided to straight out ask me the question he'd been alluding to for the last two weeks. As he put it, it was time for us to take our relationship to the next level. I had to give it to him though. He used some tact in the way he explained himself and the reasons why we should have sex.

"You know, Tonya, we've been kickin' it all summer, and all you ever let me get is a feel. Why is that?" James wanted to know.

"Should there be more than that? I ain't trying to get into any trouble, James," I said, sitting up and facing him.

"I'm not trying to get in no trouble either, especially with your crazy father," James tried to joke, "But we've got to do something other than these little kissing sessions."

"So what are you saying to me?" I asked, knowing full well what he was talking about.

"Look, I've been with plenty of girls, and you're the first one I have ever waited this long for, and a brother's got needs, 'ya know what I'm sayin?" James explained.

Needs? I was going to ask him what kind of needs, but there was no pretending that I didn't know what James was talking about. I told him a while ago that I was a virgin and didn't intend to have sex before marriage. He backed off for a while, but came right back at me with his idea. Usually just telling him this would work, but not tonight. No, tonight, I was handed an ultimatum: we either go to the next level in our relationship, or he's going to move on, it was as simple as that.

"Tonya, for real, I like you a lot and all, but Baby, I ain't no virgin. I know you never did anything, so I'll take my time with you. I'll protect you and everything, ok? For real, aiight? I promise not to hurt you…"

"And you promise not to tell all your friends?" I asked sarcastically, cutting off his list of promises I knew he had no intention of keeping.

"I never do stupid stuff like that! I respect myself and I respect my girl, you know that. Have I ever disrespected you, have I ever?" James asked.

"Well…no…"

"Then it shouldn't be no problem. I'll give you some time to think it over and then maybe one day after school we can head up to my house. Ain't nobody there until around six, and we'll be finished long before that…" James talked on and on about *our* plans. I just sat there in his arms feeling like I'd already lost my virginity. Yet I didn't have the nerve to tell him how I really felt about his ideas. No, I just sat there and listened to him tell me how much he's grown to love me, as if this would make me feel better. As if I even believed that James actually loved me! This was the first time since we had been dating that I was glad when James left to go home.

Like we had done the two previous school years, my friends and I met up to walk to school on the first day of our junior year. The morning was warm with a light breeze and the air smelled so clean, prompting me to begin to consider what I was expecting out of the coming school year. My friends and I talked all the way to school about the classes they had chosen at the end of the last school year and what teachers we hoped we would have. We had already decided not to wear any of our new school clothes the first two weeks of school because that is what the freshman and sophomore students did. Instead, we still wore shorts, short-sleeved shirts and sneakers.

At first I was glad school was back in session only because we have the best high school in the city. Our school is very small, just being built about five years before we all started high school. The older high school was way overcrowded and located on the east side of town. The parents in our community began to complain since the one high school housed students from the east side of town as well as the west side. James went to our high school because his parents used his aunt's address. My friends and I lived on the west side so we were able to attend the new high school with its pale, almost pink colored bricks.

The windows of the school went almost from the ceiling to the floor, but they were narrow. The janitors worked hard to keep those windows clean, as well as the hallways, classrooms and grounds. The floors in the hallway were swept daily and waxed every Saturday morning along with the floors in each classroom. Chalkboards covered most of the walls in the classrooms. Our supply closets were always filled with the supplies we needed for subjects such as art or home economics. Our hall lockers were a sky blue that had a compartment on the bottom and the top. The gym was state of the art, professional scoreboards for basketball, top of the line bleachers and all new gym equipment. The shrubbery on the school grounds was manicured and the grass cut to perfection. The rules for the upkeep of this three-story building were far stricter than the other high school. We had security guards on duty round the clock, brand new books, supplies, computers, and whatever one would find in a more affluent neighborhood.

My joy about returning to school quickly turned to dread, the week school was back in session, when I agreed to sleep with James. I was a nervous wreck! Every time he would see me in the hall, he would lean over and whisper little reminders and encouraging words in my ear. Or he would sneak up behind me, grabbing me as if he wanted to squeeze the life out of me and say, "It's gonna be good, Baby Girl...real good..." By the end of the week James had gotten on my nerves something fierce, and I almost told him a few times to just forget about it.

Usually classes dragged along, especially science, but that day, all of my classes flew by quickly, and the time to meet James was in my face. Instead of being at his locker like normal, he was at mine before I even got there. Dragging along and taking my time wasn't enough to hold James off. He was hurrying me along until eventually I told him I couldn't do it, I just couldn't.

James' reaction was one of shock. At first he kept trying to convince me to take that walk to his house, all the while flipping his baseball cap frontward, backwards and then frontward again. I had come to learn that James only flips that cap on his head when he becomes nervous, and sometimes when he becomes angry. He was real angry, but he didn't want me to know it until he realized that I wasn't going to budge in my decision...then he let me have it.

"I can't believe I wasted my whole summer on you! Now you want me to think you're too innocent to kick it with me? Forget you then!" James screamed in my face. "I am a playa, Girl, didn't you know that? I was just trying to turn you on to something you never had before, but it's all right. I'm straight though 'cause I can always get with someone else. Then you gonna be wanting me, girl, and I ain't gonna be having you. Peace."

I stood there feeling so stupid while James walked down the hall flashing his crooked grin at all the girls he passed. But eventually I unglued my feet from the floor, retrieved my books from my locker and headed towards home. As bad as James made me feel, I still felt good about my decision and myself.

# Chapter Three

Although the first operation was successful, my doctor recommended a second operation, using a new surgical procedure, to restructure my jaw. The surgery was scheduled just a month and a half after the first one. A plastic surgeon that specializes in facial problems would assist with the second surgery. They wanted to put my jaw back in place, like it was before my attack. Since I would be out of commission for a long time, I told my mother I wanted to get my hair cut low enough to just brush it and go. It would be easier for me to care for, but she wouldn't hear of it. She and my grandmother said they would be there to do whatever I needed, so that idea was quickly done away with.

The entire week leading up to the surgery, thoughts of how I would look after the second operation haunted me. I thought I looked deformed and ugly, and feared the surgery would make matters worse. I tried to reason with myself that it was for the best, echoing my mother's comments when my grandmother asked her if we were sure a second operation would help. My father had already made the decision and didn't answer when my grandmother started her questioning, but my mother, using her quiet manner, fielded all the questions. I retreated to my room and tried to find something to take my thoughts away from a surgery that could make me look uglier.

The morning my parents took me to the hospital, I went into the bathroom and took my time changing into the gown the nurse handed me. The doctor came in to explain to my family what they were going to do. I put on my bathrobe and sat on the end of the bed, pretending to be watching television since I was not included in their conversation.

"This is a fairly new technique we're using, but we have had no major side effects. We are going to restructure Tonya's jaw to give it the shape and contour it originally had. Her recuperating period in the hospital will be four or five days, with a few follow-up visits in my office. She'll be able to talk real soon thereafter. Tonya will also need to begin therapy after the bandages and wiring are removed."

"What are the risks with this operation?" my father asked.

"The same as with any other operation, Mr. Henderson. Anesthesia could be a risk, as well as her body not responding to or rejecting any medication. But the material we are using to restructure her jaw is very safe, and we foresee no adverse reactions or added risks."

My parents asked the doctor more questions and talked as if I wasn't there. I could have cared less about the procedure and the things they were planning to do to me, but what concerned me was that no one bothered to ask me how I felt about it, or if I even wanted the second operation. I'm not vain and I did want my face back. Actually I wanted the operation, but I didn't want my parents to have full say in what was to happen to me and when.

I found it hard to go to sleep the evening before the surgery, and just as I began to doze off at five a.m. the following morning, a nurse came in talking to me as if the sun was already up. She explained that I would be given a shot to make me drowsy, and as soon as the medicine took effect, I would be wheeled to the operating room. When the nurse left to get the needle, I went into the bathroom to wash my face to try and quell the sudden nervousness that welled up in me. For some reason I felt that once I was put to sleep, I would not wake up. By the time I came out of the bathroom, my forehead and top lip had beads of sweat on them and I couldn't sit down.

The nurse returned as promised, to administer the shot and stayed with me until the orderlies came to wheel me to the operating room. By then, the medicine had already begun to relax me and the nervousness was gone. I lay there trying to think of something happy, but I couldn't. Instead I closed my eyes and tried to block out the sounds of the nurses and the doctor, the insertion of the I.V., hissing of the blood pressure cuff and the bleeps of the heart monitor. I heard the doctor say, "Let us begin..." as I drifted into complete darkness.

When I woke up, I was in a large room lined with hospital beds on both sides. Once my eyes adjusted to the light, I tried to move, but my head started to spin so I quickly lay back down. Before long the surgeon checked on me just before I was taken back to my hospital room, assuring me that the operation was successful. At that moment I was too groggy to really make heads or tails of our one-sided conversation, but I understood the word "successful." My parents and grandparents were in the room waiting for me. They showered me with the love and attention they thought I needed. All I really wanted was to be left alone for the next four days that I would be in the hospital. Seeing all of them there made me wish for home so that my grandparents would eventually leave. Dealing with my parents was hard enough because they treated me as if I was still five years old and couldn't make any decisions on my own. Whatever the doctor said, they pretty much agreed with it, without ever considering that I might disagree. But to avoid any unnecessary problems, I just sat there as if I was totally detached from my own situation.

Although I knew how many days I would be in the hospital following the surgery, I felt like I would go crazy in that hospital room.

The only visitors I had were family members. The constant traffic of nurses changing my bandages and checking my vitals had gotten on my nerves! Watching television was far from entertaining, and the books and magazines my mother brought me didn't hold my interest. When my doctor came to my room four days after the surgery and told me he was releasing me, I could have danced around my room. He sent me home with instructions on how to clean the site of the surgery and change the bandages.

My first day home, I was sitting in the den with my mouth wired shut again, lips constantly feeling dry, and a bandage covering my face when the doorbell rang. My mother answered the door and I heard her telling Lisa where I was. Lisa's hurried footsteps sounded in the hall as she made her way to the den.

"Hey, Tonya! What's up, Girl?" Lisa screamed as soon as she walked into the den, grabbing me and holding me in a tight hug.

I returned Lisa's hug, smiling as best I could; I was so glad to see her. I had been so caught up in myself that I'd completely forgotten school was out.

Lisa told me that Sasha and Denise were on their way over, and explained Denise had not come by because she couldn't handle seeing me like this. Lisa waved her hand making light of Denise's excuse as she took a seat next to me on the sofa, asking me when I would be getting the bandage off, and asking questions about my attack. Just why did the attack happen, but before she could finish, I was hanging my head in shame and Lisa was offering her apologies and soon she fell silent.

Lisa's discomfort caused her to fiddle with the bottom of her skirt. That's when I realized she actually had one on. Lisa, who wore nothing but pants and jeans, had on a skirt, a nice pair of sandals and a shirt that revealed her belly button! Not only that! She must have lost about a good thirty pounds and no longer sported her messy tomboy ponytail. It was permed and styled into a short bob with one side tucked behind her ear. The only time Lisa would do something nice to her hair was on a special occasion. I was really surprised at the change in my friend, but she looked really good.

I didn't want Lisa to feel too bad about the questions she asked me, so I made an effort to change the subject and lighten the air. Scribbling Lisa a note on my pad, I asked her about her new boyfriend and her plans for her final year in college. I really wanted to ask her about the skirt, but I figured it would be better to ask that question when I was able to talk.

"My boyfriend is treating me all right. Next year is my last year, so I have to decide what I want to do. He will be continuing and will be doing his internship at a hospital in L.A., so I might be staying there after graduation."

While Lisa and I were catching up, Sasha and Denise arrived. It seemed like forever since I'd seen Sasha. I started crying as soon as she walked into the den.

"Oh, Tonya, please don't cry! I miss you too, Girl," Sasha said, wiping my tears with her fingers while pushing away a few strands of hair and I immediately noticed that she allowed her hair to grow. I was used to seeing Sasha with a close cut haircut, so to see her hair fall in her face was a nice surprise. She had put on a little weight as well, and was looking better than I'd ever seen her look.

Denise apologized for not coming sooner saying she didn't know what to expect, but I cut off her words by squeezing her hand, trying to assure her that I understood with my eyes. Denise and I stayed in contact with each other the most since we were the only two who did not go away to school. I understood why she might have a problem talking to me, especially if she wasn't sure of what state I would be in mentally and physically. Denise had grown out of her shyness, but she was still a little standoffish when it came to things she didn't quite understand. My mother added her own flavor to the mix by giving them a slice of her yellow cake with chocolate frosting. To help the healing process, my mouth was wired shut, so I had to sip my lunch. I wished I could have traded mouths with them for a slice of Mom's cake. It wasn't long before they left with promises to be back soon. Feeling tired from their visit, I fell off to sleep on the sofa.

• • •

Since the attack and returning home, I had started to have terrible dreams. Although they didn't come as often, I started having one during the nap. First the wicked laugh taunted me, coming and going in different directions; in a low tone and then in loud tones, giving me a feeling of running with no place to hide, the laugh ricocheting all around me. But this time the visions in my dream were a little clearer with the face starting out being normal, but then it quickly morphed, his skin changing to a deep black color. The pupils in his eyes turned red with thin yellow slits, and his teeth seemed to grow five inches and hang out of his mouth with a lot of saliva. I felt completely trapped, the sound of my heart beating erratically in my ears, and the sound of his wicked laugh echoing in my head.

I awoke screaming and gagging, sweat pouring while I was actually in motion to run. My mother was immediately at my side comforting and reassuring me that I was safe and no harm would come to me. She took the hand towel she kept in the pocket of her apron and wiped the sweat and tears that continued to pour even after she wiped my face. Burying my head in her bosom, I cried like a little child, deep sobs until the

45

crying ceased and there was nothing left by dry heaves and an occasional tear.

Realizing that my crying had come to an end, my mother wiped my face once again and helped me to settle myself again on the sofa. Suddenly feeling totally naked and cold, I grabbed my blanket and wrapped it tightly around my legs. I was still sleepy, but I refused to go back to sleep, wanting to avoid another nightmare. So in an attempt to take my mind off of the dream, I turned the TV on, flipping from one station to another. I avoided talk shows, for fear they would do a topic similar to my situation. I never enjoyed soap operas, so I bypassed these as well. When I couldn't find anything I wanted to watch, I turned the TV off and sat up with some pillows behind me to make sure I didn't fall asleep.

Needing something else to divert my attention, I purposely began to reminisce about the past and my relationship with my friends. We haven't spent a lot of time together since high school, but I still valued their friendship just as much, if not more. Lisa was my strength and confidant, while Denise was the one who became the voice of reason and logic, and Sasha was hard to describe in just a word or two. It was Sasha who I thought about in particular because it had been such a long time since I'd seen her.

Thinking about Sasha would normally bring a smile to my face, so I settled for the comfort of my thoughts. She may have a lot of mouth, but she has a big caring heart. In spite of all her troubles, she managed to keep us laughing, especially when she was checking out guys and cracking her gum in between her words. No doubt Sasha had her own take on the world and life, and seemed to live hers to the fullest with a few extras to boot. And she always had a plan to do something, or figure out a way for us to be cool and make our classmates jealous. Yeah, I think if Lisa and I were not best friends, Sasha and I would have been, once I got over her witty tongue and bold attitude. Resting my head on the back of the sofa, I couldn't help wishing I possessed some of Sasha's characteristics. Maybe things in my life would be different.

# Chapter Four

The bandages and the wiring in my jaw came off a few weeks later. I made my first attempts at speaking, and felt awkward and clumsy because I couldn't open my mouth all the way. The doctor scheduled therapy sessions to help me get used to using my jaw to talk and chew, and recommended I see a therapist to talk about what happened to me. I refused, convincing my parents and myself that I didn't need it. Why should I talk about what happened to me with a complete stranger? It wouldn't change anything.

Just knowing that I would need therapy to improve my speech convinced me that I couldn't function outside of the confines of my home. Not that my speech was impaired, but I felt like everyone would be able to tell that I was having a little difficulty and would treat me accordingly. Not only did the damage to my face serve as a reminder and a public show of my attack but talking confirmed that I had a problem. Since I didn't know how to handle that, I made sure I stayed home away from people as much as possible.

I had put singing and any plans to make it a career totally out of my mind until my mother brought it up the day doctor removed the wiring from my mouth. I decided to go into the kitchen while she prepared dinner, hoping she would be good company and share some good conversation. I could smell the meatloaf she had baking in the oven. My mouth watered in anticipation of my first taste of solid food. My mother was at the stove stirring the mashed potatoes with a wooden spoon while adding some black pepper.

"Mom, I hope you saved me some cake," I said, taking a seat at the kitchen table.

"You need a good, home cooked meal," Mom answered, turning the pots off while I started to set the table. My father had called earlier to say he would be working late, so my mother and I ate at the kitchen table.

My mother's meatloaf was seasoned to perfection with peas on the side, mashed potatoes and applesauce, all of it soft food. I had been eating applesauce so long that I almost choked on it.

"Everything tastes good, Mom. Maybe I'll cook dinner tomorrow night."

"Really? So tell me something; are you planning to stay in the house and cook, or have you given any thought to going back to school?" my mother asked as she placed her fork beside her plate.

"No...what I mean is, I haven't given it much thought," I said while avoiding her eyes.

"Are you going to try to sing any? I don't mean with that group again, I'm talking about at church," Mom said, taking a seat and sipping from her cup of tea at the same time.

"No, Mom. I don't want to anymore."

"Don't let this stop you, Tonya," my mother said, making eye contact with me.

"Not right now, okay? Singing is what caused this problem in the first place."

"Baby, you can't let this incident take away your gift to sing..."

"No, Mom, please! I don't want to talk about it, ok?" There was no way I wanted to think about singing when I had to make a conscious effort to pronounce my words. I reasoned with her but with a hint of finality in my voice, cutting off any further conversation about singing.

"I'm sorry. Do you want that piece of cake now?" my mother asked, obviously getting the hint.

"Yes..."

My mother's questions made me really begin to think about what I was going to do with myself. I still refused to think too much about a career, but I figured now that the bandage and wiring was gone, the least I could do was attend church on Sunday. I still didn't like to go anywhere unless I had to. At first, my girls would come and check on me a couple times a week, almost begging me to go to the movies or the mall. Sasha was the main one. She called me almost every day, trying to convince me to at least go for a car ride, but I would always refuse. She tried her best to convince me using her own personal tragedy to encourage me, reminding me of how I helped her when she needed me the most. But I wasn't up to it and I figured that I might as well stay within the confines of my temporary protection, in the house with my parents. Besides that, my face still had some spots that needed to heal, so I couldn't bring myself to go out. The only place I would go was to church and back home on Sunday. That alone was hard enough.

Out of all of my friends, it was Sasha who made it by my house to check on me. She came by two or three times a week, even if it was just to see how I was doing. Somehow she was able to get past my moody and negative attitude and see about me, trying her best to encourage me, reminding me of my faithful friendship to her in her time of need. Truthfully, I was surprised that it wasn't Lisa who was there for me constantly since she lived directly across the street.

Now that I think about it, Sasha was also there for me in the past, even when I broke up with James. Sasha was the one to approach James first, introducing him to the rest of us. In spite of this, she still moved out of the way to allow my first real relationship with a boy to blossom.

When James and I broke up, she even took part in the game Lisa, Denise and I started by keeping track of James' girlfriends; at least a different girl every other day or so. He was so weak! I guess he wanted to prove he was really a "playa." Sasha was on my side.

That is until the day I saw James walking down the hall with his arm around Sasha. I really wanted to scream through the halls, or throw my books to the floor, but instead I just rolled my eyes hard at the both of them and went on to my next class. When I saw Sasha later that morning, I walked right past her and kept walking even though she was screaming my name at the top of her lungs. I sure wasn't speaking to Sasha after this dumb move. Then she had the nerve to come and sit at our table in the cafeteria like nothing ever happened!

At first I started not to say anything, just blow it off, but I couldn't help it. Sasha came to the table talking to me as if all was well. I pushed my tray away from me, turned to Sasha and stared at her without saying a word.

"What?" Sasha asked, pushing a few fries in her mouth.

"You and James kickin' it now?" I wanted to know.

"Oh, Girl, please! You trippin'! He's all right though, I like his style," Sasha said, taking a big bite from her burger.

"How can you even talk to James when you know what happened between us?" I asked her, pulling my tray of food back in front of me.

"Why should my friendship with James have anything to do with you? Just because you couldn't keep him don't mean he ain't free to talk to whoever he wants," Sasha said nonchalantly, taking a sip of her chocolate milk.

"Oh, so it's like that?" I asked, again pushing my food away as I felt the heat of my anger rise.

"Yep, it's like that. Come on, Tonya, you have to admit he is kinda irresistible and cute…plus, he can dress, and you know how much I like that," Sasha explained, eating a few more fries. "Besides, we were just talking. I let him put his arm around me so he can feel like the player he thinks he is, 'cause he sure ain't."

I wondered if Sasha took anything seriously. With all the drama she's had to grow up with, it's a miracle the girl is not in a mental institution. From the time I met Sasha when we were on the playground the summer before our freshman year of high school, I couldn't understand how her mother could afford to live on the west side of town. She was a straight-up alcoholic, and a prostitute. Not that Sasha's mother stood on the corner soliciting, but different men would come to her house all the time for "favors." That was her way of keeping a roof over Sasha's head, clothes on her back, and a little food in the house. There were also a few times when Sasha was approached by a few of the men who visited her mother, but her mother wouldn't allow it to happen, thank God.

I had spent the night over Sasha's house a few times until Lisa's mother told mine about Sasha's home situation. The only thing I ever witnessed was her mother's drinking and one guy who visited and stayed in the living room. But it was Sasha who told me that her mother had sex with different men to support them and her drinking habit. This kind of life didn't allow Sasha to have a close relationship with her mother at all.

Sasha McPherson is not just cute; she is down right pretty. Always sporting a cute, close cut hair do with tight curls that are always in place, a very petite but shapely body, and a big, smart mouth. I've often marveled at how loud Sasha was and yet be so tiny. Petite with flawless, creamy brown skin, Sasha knew she was a cutie and she let everyone else know it too.

Sasha's explanation about her encounter with James calmed my suspicions by the time Lisa and Denise made it to our table. Lunch was almost over, so our time to catch up on the latest gossip was cut virtually in half. But I still held the memory of Sasha and James in my mind because, for some reason, it didn't sit too well with me. Every now and then I had to take a shot to see where Sasha's head really was concerning James.

Knowing James the way I did, I was a little afraid for Sasha and mad that James chose to try to talk to one of my friends. By the time the bell rang for our next class, I decided to dismiss the incident altogether. Besides, Sasha was a flirt, so there was no need to worry myself crazy about it. Plus James and I had broken up six months earlier and I was over him.

By the time the bell rang to go to our next class, we had already made plans to walk home together and then hang out at my house after school to come up with something to do once we completed our homework. I sat in my last period class trying to come up with something we could do other than hang out at my house instead of concentrating on History. By the time the dismissal bell rang, I was ready with my suggestions and ran them by my friends as we headed towards my house and my room to get our homework done and out of the way so we could do something we enjoyed. I looked forward to these times with my friends because I wasn't allowed to go anywhere for any length of time unless there was no school the next day, it was a Saturday, or summer vacation. So right after school, my friends and I headed to my house

One of the advantages of being an only child was I didn't have to share my room with anyone, and I had just about everything in there. My room was in the front right corner of the house, so I caught the early morning sunlight through the sheer, white curtains. I had a closet almost the full length of the room to keep all my clothes and so many boxes of shoes that I had lost count.

My oak canopy bed was positioned against the wall, directly across from the windows. The canopy matched the sheer curtains at the window. I had two matching nightstands, one to hold my telephone, and the other for my clock and whatever. I kept all of my electronics against the wall closest to the door; my sound system was tight, but the only time I could listen to secular music or anything but gospel or church music was when I put on my earphones because my parents would have a fit if they knew. It was also equipped with a CD and tape player. Next to that I was able to squeeze a small desk for my computer and printer.

Right in front of my windows, I had three big blue beanbags so that my friends had something to sit on when they came up to my room. The rug on my floor was a pale blue, as well as the walls, with white trim around the doors and windows. Lisa and Denise took a seat in the beanbags while Sasha sat on the floor in between them. I sat in the other beanbag chair while we tried to plan what we were going to do after we finished our homework.

"We can always go to the courts," Denise was saying, as she handed me a pen from her book bag.

"No, the courts are getting tired. Besides that, we know all the guys who hang out down there already," Lisa said, leaning back in her beanbag.

"Uh uh, no, we can't hang out down there too much. It's always the same old...the same old people doing the same old things anyway. But then again, some of us got a curfew...gotta be in when the street lights come on," Sasha said, chuckling and nudging Lisa.

"Oh, shut up, Sasha! What do you want to do since you have so much to say?" I said to take the attention away from me.

"Well, let me see...we can go to the mall! I bet you we'll see some new guys, right Lisa?" Sasha said, looking to Lisa for confirmation.

"Yeah, we could! I wanna get a new CD with my allowance, plus there are some new stores open."

It turned out that we had a special youth meeting at church that night, so my mother quickly cancelled the mall visit. A Tuesday night at that, and there was no way I could talk my way out of it if I tried. Mom said it concerned the youth, so I had to go, never mind it was being held on a night that we don't normally have church service.

"See, I knew I shouldn't have tried to go anywhere on a school night...especially with somebody who can't hang," Sasha said while she put her books back in her book bag.

"Excuse you?" I said, looking at Sasha with my left eyebrow raised.

"Squash it, Tonya," Lisa said. "We can go Saturday or something."

"I think that would be better," Denise added.

After I walked my friends to the door, I watched them split up once they reached the sidewalk in front of my house, each heading for her home. I went back upstairs to get ready to go to church with my parents.

Both of my parents were raised in the church and they were bent on bringing me up the same way, which my father believed would help him control my life. Well, my father and God, so *he* says. It seemed as if my parent's commitment to church had a lot to do with the length of time they have been in the church. Dad had to hurry to be on time because he is the Chairman of the Deacon Board. He handles the finances and any other duty Pastor asks of him. Mom, in her quiet way, has helped many of our members, so she stressed the importance of being there on time as well.

"Tonya, come on. Your father is already in the car," my mother said on her way out the door.

"I'm coming!" I said, stomping down the stairs, thinking dag! I hate it when I plan to stay home or go somewhere else and some church activity comes up. I wanted to go chill with my girls.

When we arrived at the church, the parking lot was almost full and there were cars I didn't recognize. I could feel that there was something funky going on and that whatever it was it required full attendance from the members of our church and community.

After getting everyone's attention and calling order to the meeting, Pastor Jackson began to speak. We could all see that he was really upset because he kept wiping at his face with his handkerchief. As I looked around, I saw faces I'd never seen before, and our principal and school nurse sat in the podium area with Pastor Jackson. Oh something real funky was definitely going on. It was very quiet as Pastor Jackson began talking, his voice choked with emotion as he explained why we were there.

"My heart is aching for the reason of this meeting. If it were at all possible, we wouldn't be gathering here for such a time as this. I'm not here just to tell you we have lost someone to death, but that the loss of a few of our young people is due to the epidemic of AIDS. Now it has hit us here at our own church...one of our young teenagers has contracted the disease," Pastor Jackson began, taking a handkerchief from his pocket to wipe the two streams of tears that started down his cheeks.

On and on Pastor Jackson went about AIDS, the epidemic proportions it has risen to among young people my age and some younger ones, and the fact that it is touching all of our lives directly or indirectly. He summed up his sermon with just a few more words. "I call AIDS a death sentence or punishment fitting the crime because we know that the God we serve can reverse and heal any disease, just like in the case of an actual death sentence in jail that can be reversed. I call it a "death wish" for anyone who dabbles in sex outside of marriage because you've knowingly taken the opportunity to invite death into your lives."

Pastor Jackson spoke for a few more minutes, wiping an occasional tear as he talked. By the time he was through, quite a few of us were wiping tears. Although our Pastor is a big man, about six, five, weighing close to three hundred pounds, I didn't think he was wimp or something because he cried. His close cut haircut only served to show all the wrinkles on his forehead when he talked about serious matters, while his big hands demonstrated the pain he felt in his heart as he held his hand to his chest when he spoke.

Afterward Pastor presented our principal and school nurse to discuss the issue of AIDS in our school. They also left instructions and pamphlets for those who have been sexually active to have testing done. They were also working closely with the two clinics in town to educate us all about this fatal disease. We were told that counselors would be sent to the school to talk to those who needed it. They would be working collectively but confidentially with those who have been diagnosed so they can give names of the individuals they were involved with sexually. This way those people could be notified of the possibility of having the disease themselves.

Although Pastor Jackson chose not to reveal who had actually contracted AIDS, I started running down people my age in my mind. By the time we left church that night, I'd narrowed it down to a few possibilities. This information was based on the all the girls that I knew who were fast, as my mother called them. But then I thought about the possibility of it being a guy, and I added about three of them to my list of possibilities.

• • •

A few weeks after the meeting at church, the whispering had started around school and town. The HIV/AIDS virus was the talk of our community and our high school with people making assumptions about anyone they felt messed around with too many people. Since a lot of people had limited knowledge of just how the disease was contracted, the symptoms or how a person was supposed to look who had it, they were afraid to even touch a stranger's hand. By the time May rolled around, our school was in a total uproar. A few fights broke out as girls and guys alike defended themselves and their reputations amidst all of the rumors. The counselors did come, but in spite of the promise of confidentiality, rumors, whether true or false, were flying around like crazy.

One day my girls and I were having lunch and fooling around as usual when James walked by. At first we just watched him, and after he'd gone by, we burst out laughing, not caring that he heard us. James had not been hanging around the girls as much as he did before, and he had been looking like he lost his best friend. Good! One of the rumors going around school was James was HIV positive. The rumors stopped him from being the "playa-playa" he claimed to be.

While we decided to talk about the hot issue, some girl came to our table. Nobody said anything at first. We just looked at her as if she were crossing territory lines. Then our spokesperson, Lisa, checked her right quick.

"So what's up? You want something?" Lisa asked, looking her up and down and then up and down again.

"Yeah, if you don't mind, I want to tell you all something."

"What?" Lisa asked, eyeing her suspiciously.

"Look, I'mma just say this, ok? James Barnett is one of the fools going around here spreading HIV! I know he over there trying to see if

I'm telling what I know, but yeah...I'm telling it. Only because I know you used to kick it with him," the girl said, touching me lightly on my arm.

The girl let us know what was going on with the HIV situation at our school, stating that James was one of the main ones spreading the disease. She had been tested and was awaiting her results, but felt the least she could do was tell as many people she could about it.

"Can you get it from kissing?" Denise asked. "I heard that you could."

"I don't know..." the girl answered.

"That's messed up," Lisa said, shaking her head.

Then Sasha stood up suddenly and said she had to get to her next class to see her teacher before class started. Before either of us could ask why, she was already headed towards the door.

For the rest of the day I found it hard to concentrate in my classes after hearing about James and his HIV status. Most of those thoughts started with "what if..." Although I was glad I didn't have sex with James, I was still a little shook when I realized that I had considered sleeping with James, and would have if I hadn't come to my senses. I was thankful when the last bell of the day rang so I could meet up with Lisa and head home, but that didn't end the discussion about James or the one we had at lunch.

As we were walking home, all of a sudden someone came up behind us at the corner from my house and put their hands on my eyes. As soon as I smelled the Halston cologne, I knew it was James.

"You can take your hands off my eyes, James," I said, with no emotion in my voice.

"Oh, so you know it's me then? What's up? How you doing, Lisa?" James said, flipping that stupid baseball cap like he usually does.

"I'm all right," Lisa said, turning away from James.

"What do you want, James? I thought you weren't speaking to me anymore," I said, looking him up and down.

"I was trying to give you some space. I ain't coldhearted, Tonya. I was just mad 'cause we couldn't kick it in a special way," he explained.

"The only way we're going to kick it is *hi and bye*," I said, holding eye contact with James.

"I know that's right," Lisa said, standing beside me now.

"This is between me and Tonya, Lisa," James said, with his cap frozen in the middle of one of his flips.

"So what? And I'm talking to you, James," Lisa said, not backing down.

"At least let me walk you home. I don't want to come in," James said, ignoring Lisa's last comment.

"You wasn't coming in anyway!" I said, wishing he would just go away. Lisa and I continued to walk and James fell in step right behind us. I didn't know why I let him walk me home. Lisa gave me a quick elbow to the ribs just as this thought occurred to me, but she didn't cross the street to her house. Instead, she walked right along with me.

"So what's been up with you?" James asked.

"Nothing..." What if someone from school saw me walking with James? The rumors would include me and I don't know how I would handle that, I thought to myself. After a few moments of silence, James walked closer and bumped me as if we were still good friends. I glared at him without saying a word.

"Oh what, we're not cool?"

"No, she's not cool with you," Lisa said answering for me. We had just reached the sidewalk in front of my house. My mother opened the door. Lisa spoke and made a quick getaway towards home, leaving me to deal with my mother's serious look alone. She stood there with her hands on both hips, tapping her foot, so I knew it was more than just me leaving the milk out that morning in my rush to meet my friends.

"Hey, how you doin', Mrs. Henderson?" James said to my mother.

"I'm fine…how are you, James?" my mother replied. I could tell that she was really heated by the short response she gave James.

"I'm aiight. Tonya, I'll see you in school tomorrow," James said, tapping me on my shoulder before he headed down the street. I didn't respond because my mother had that, "wait until you get in this house" look on her face. My mother held the door open for me and I could almost feel her wrath before she ever opened her mouth.

"I want you to put those books down and come listen to this answering machine," my mother said before I could get through the hallway.

*What did I do now?* I thought to myself. I know when Mom is p'd about something, so I was quick about doing what she said.

"Yes, Mom?" I asked, trying to look as innocent as I could when I walked in the den.

"I want you to hear what was on the answering machine this afternoon when I got home," my mother said pressing the button so I could hear the recording. The person who left the message addressed me as one of James' ho's and asked had I gotten the package from him.

After hearing that message, I knew I was in big trouble. My mother launched right into her lecture and threats concerning my dealings with James and the things we heard at church. My mother replaced her usual calm manner of handling serious matters, with a chorus of advice and what she would do if, and wait until my father came home. My attempts at trying to defend myself were useless because my mother was on a roll.

I sat there and took my verbal punishment until my mother dismissed me with her final words:

"Kids and sex today! It makes absolutely no sense to just sleep around without at least taking some kind of precaution."

Mom was trippin' that day. If she knew how close I'd come to having sex with James, I would be getting ready for my own funeral right now, 'cause Mom would kill me long before AIDS ever could. When my father came home, it was far worse than I could have imagined. He threatened to go to James' house to talk to his parents, and a host of other off the wall things he could possibly think of. Even locking me in my room every day after school! I just sat there and listened to him real good, something I haven't done in a very long time. Only because I realized more than ever that making the right decision kept me from getting into more trouble than either of us could ever handle.

Once my parents said how they felt about the James situation and anything about sex and sexually transmitted diseases, I was careful about what I talked about at the dinner table for a few weeks. Sometimes the things they heard on the news could spark an evening of talk about morals and how they were raised. I didn't know just how much longer I could take hearing that. I was thankful that as the weeks leading up to the end of school went by, the talk at our dining room table shifted to conversations other than questionable morals and bad choices.

With school about to end for the summer, we were all excited about it and the possibilities of finding something new to do. I was hoping it wouldn't be like last summer because it was just too boring. Well, with the exception of meeting guys, but I didn't want to do that the summer leading up to my senior year in high school, especially after all the talk about sexually transmitted diseases.

Ever since the rumors about James and AIDS were confirmed, Sasha became unusually quiet. We all tried to get to the bottom of her problem, but she wouldn't let us, and started separating herself from us, disappearing every day after finals saying she was tired and wanted to just go home. No matter how hard we tried, Sasha would not open up and tell us what was bothering her.

Right after the finals, I received a letter in the mail from Sasha. I couldn't understand why she would mail me a letter when we see each other every day. It didn't have a return address, but I knew it was mailed locally because of the meter stamp on the envelope. My thoughts were that it was a chain letter, so my first reaction was to just throw it in the trashcan. Then I noticed a smiley face sticker on the back keeping the letter closed. The only person I knew who used these stickers for everything was Sasha. I tore into the envelope, tearing a corner of the letter.

> *Hey, Tonya. I'm sorry I haven't been myself lately, but it's hard to do that when you have so much on your mind. Well, really it's one thing. Whoever says teens don't have problems has never met me, right? You're supposed to laugh at that, it was a joke, DUH! (smile)*
>
> *I love you,* Sasha

I read the letter over about five times and then picked up the phone and called Lisa. *Just what in the world did all of this mess mean?* While Lisa's phone rang, I read it over quickly once again. I couldn't make out what Sasha was trying to tell me in her letter other than she had problems, but what problems didn't we already know about? Lisa finally answered and I launched into my reason for calling.

"What? Wait a minute! Let me come over there so I can read this letter," Lisa said, slamming the phone down. I ran downstairs and paced in front of the door until I saw Lisa coming across the street. I didn't wait for her to ring the doorbell, I met her on the porch, and we read the letter together.

"What should we do, Lisa? Sasha has really been depressed lately, and it's no telling what is on her mind," I reasoned.

"Want to go by her house? I'm going to ask her straight out what's going on with her 'cause I ain't trying to figure out no riddle in no letter. For all we know, this is just another tactic for her to get attention," Lisa said, handing the letter back to me.

Calling to my mother through the screen door, I said, "Mom, may I go with Lisa over to Sasha's house?" My mother said I could, but I had to be back in time for dinner, so Lisa and I walked around the corner to her house. Lisa complained almost all the way to Sasha's house about Sasha's antics and crazy things she would do to get attention.

"I know one thing, if Sasha is just playing around, I'mma...I don't know what I'm gonna do, but I'm gonna do something to her," Lisa said as we approached Sasha's house. Since we didn't like going through Sasha's mother, we knocked on Sasha's window several times, but she didn't answer.

"Wanna knock on the door? I'll do it so you don't have to say anything to her mother. I don't know why you're so scared of her," Lisa said, heading towards the front door without giving me a chance to protest.

Sasha and her mother rented the first floor of a two-family home. I was really hoping her mother would be out, but no sooner than the doorbell rang once, Sasha's mother appeared.

"Hi girls," Ms. McPherson said, staggering and holding on to the frame of the door. "Come on in...Sasha's in her room. Tell her I said come and do those dishes before she goes anywhere."

We nodded and hurried to Sasha's room. After knocking a few times, I tried the door and it was open, so we went right on in. Sasha was covered with a comforter, her fan turned off and her window closed on an eighty-five degree day. I went over and shook her, but she wouldn't wake up.

"All right Sasha, game's over! Get your lazy butt up and go do those dishes like your mother said," Lisa said, giving Sasha a hard shove.

I snatched the covers off, and Sasha's arm hung from the bed with a prescription bottle in it. I took it and found that there were no pills left in the bottle. I just started screaming. The screaming brought Sasha's mother stumbling back to the bedroom. Sasha couldn't wake up because it appeared she had swallowed a bottle of her mother's prescription painkillers.

The rest of the events that followed were a blur to me. I couldn't move from the spot where I stood next to Sasha's bed. I heard Lisa calling 911 while it seemed Ms. McPherson sobered up enough to get a cold washcloth from the bathroom to put on Sasha's head. She kept calling her name, but Sasha never moved.

As soon the ambulance arrived, Lisa and I stood back and watched as one of the attendants checked her pulse and said she was still alive. The ambulance attendants hooked up the I.V. and oxygen, along with what looked like something to monitor her heart. Sasha's mother gave them the empty pill bottle, and before we knew anything, they had Sasha on the gurney headed out the front door. Lisa and I followed and watched as the ambulance pulled away from the curb with Ms. McPherson inside holding Sasha's hand.

Lisa and I turned and walked away just as the ambulance turned a corner with the sirens fading as it went. We walked slowly down the street headed for our homes. I was feeling completely numb, almost like what I had just seen was a dream. The only words that past between me and Lisa was when she asked in a low voice, "You all right?" No, I wasn't all right, not at all. I couldn't believe that Sasha wanted to kill herself. I guess this is one time she didn't do something just to get attention. At least not the type she sought for in the past.

We walked the rest of the way home, not speaking another word to each other until we reached my house and Lisa headed across the street to her house. I went into my house and laid across my bed to think about what had just happened. The only thing I could think of was *why?*

# Chapter Five

Ever since the bandages came off, I would cross off the days on the calendar in my room as if I were counting down the days for some big event. Thirty days had gone by and all I did was stay holed up in the house, unwilling to face my fears. The longer I put off coming to terms with the attack, the more I wanted to hide away in the house. When my mouth was wired shut, I desired to talk to my best friend Lisa on the phone, but now that I could talk, I retreated further into myself, not receiving phone calls or even going out on the porch to collect the mail. It got to the point where my friends came by less and less, and the phone calls began to wane.

One friend who would not give up on me entirely was Gary Simmons. He would call me at least twice a week. Sometimes I would take his calls, and other times I wouldn't. At first when Gary called, he would apologize to me as if what happened to me was his fault. When I told him I wasn't going to talk to him anymore if he kept apologizing, Gary promised he wouldn't say that he felt responsible.

On one of my lowest days the phone rang. My mother extended the receiver to me and told me it was Gary on the other end.

"Yes?"

"Hey, Tonya. I was thinking about you. How are you doing?"

"I'm alright," I said, trying to sound like I didn't want to be bothered.

"Feeling up to seeing a movie or going to dinner?"

"No."

"Mind if I come by then?"

"If you want."

"On my way. 'Bye."

"'Bye," I said, placing the phone back on the cradle.

I went to my bedroom, quickly removed my nightgown and put on a pair of old jeans and a T-shirt, then returned to the den to wait for Gary. It didn't take him long to get here. He kissed me on my good cheek and sat down beside me. In spite of how I was feeling, I couldn't help but notice how good he smelled. I stole quick glances at him, noticing how mature he looked. Gary was an even six feet, had his hair cut down and twisted, the beginnings of dreadlocks, a switch from the braids he used to sport. He had also changed cologne, to one with a more masculine scent.

"You're looking good," Gary said, searching my face.

"Yeah right," I said, rolling my eyes at him.

"You really are," Gary said, pulling his right leg up to rest on his left knee.

"Whatever. What are you up to today?" I was suddenly feeling embarrassed by my dress down appearance compared to Gary's business casual look.

"Nothing. I cleared my day so we can do something together."

"I wish you would stop asking me out. I won't be going anywhere for a while," I said, pulling my legs under me.

"You can't camp out in the house for the rest of your life. I know what happened to you was real bad, but Tonya, life goes on." Gary was speaking softly as if trying to convince both of us with his statement.

"Yeah, it does, doesn't it?" was my weak response.

"Let's go sit on the porch."

"Maybe later when it's dark."

"I don't believe this...go get your mirror, Tonya."

"What for?"

"Just go get it. Please?"

I went across the hall to the bathroom and brought the mirror to the den and handed it to Gary. He took the mirror, looked at himself and started grooming his mustache with his hand.

"Some people, I tell you..." I said, smiling at Gary acting silly. He's always had a way to make me smile or laugh, and I had to admit to myself that it actually felt good.

"Take this mirror and look at yourself, Tonya," Gary said, handing the mirror back to me.

"I see myself when I wash my face. That's more than enough," I said, pretending to pay attention to the TV.

"I want you to look at yourself and tell me what you see," Gary encouraged.

I took the mirror and looked at myself. All I saw was a thin line where the second operation was performed. It did look much better than the first one, and since I was using vitamin E on the scar, it had faded considerably and didn't look so bad.

"What about it?" I asked.

"You are still a beautiful young lady. What a person sees on the outside can't half define what's on the inside. If your scars remained ugly and the operations didn't help, you are still the same beautiful person I've come to know."

"Are you trying to convince me you weren't attracted to me because of my looks?" I asked, hoping Gary could hear that I didn't believe him.

"That's only a part of you. I always thought you were a cutey, but when I got to really know you, that's when I fell for you. Not your face, your cute shape, your pretty hair...I fell for you. The person who lives inside of this body," Gary said, poking me in the chest for emphasis. "If that changes, it's because you allow it to change."

I set the mirror down on the table and pondered what Gary said. The thing I was most conscious of is how other people will look at me, something I was never concerned about before the attack. If I could only get past that, I would be all right, maybe.

"I understand what you're saying, but this scar will always remind me of what happened. When I look at myself, I feel like I'm what I see. Damaged. All that I was is gone for good." My lips were trembling.

Gary took my hand, his eyes glazing over with tears prompting me to turn away before I began to cry myself. "Tonya, you know how I feel about you. It doesn't matter to me that you have a scar, it's about you…everything about you. The complete package. If I could make time go back, I would have given our relationship a chance to grow. Somehow I feel like I could have protected you. But you are my heart and you will always be."

I cried then because he made me feel so beautiful, so special.

Gary wasn't able to visit as often as I would have liked, but sometimes it helped to think about him, how we met and the things we had gone through together up until that point.

• • •

When our senior year started, I hoped that this new change in our lives would help us cope with Sasha's illness better. We were conflicted on how we would deal with the retorts and glares of our peers, or how to deal with Sasha's feelings as she came to terms with her illness. Sasha's suicide attempt and illness drastically changed the way we viewed ourselves. In a roundabout way, we were focused on what we would do after graduation that we didn't plan on taking our senior year seriously. That was my plan until I had to take Child Care again.

Getting our driver's license served as a distraction for us. Except for Sasha, a car was high on our list of *must haves*. I tunneled a lot of my energy and thoughts toward convincing my father to buy me one. My father decided that I was ready to handle the responsibility for a car, so on my seventeenth birthday, November fourteenth, he bought me a car! I had been dropping hints, like cutting out pictures of a Lexus, a Beamer or a Jaguar, leaving them by his plate at the dinner table. I knew full well he wouldn't even consider buying either of these, but it helped my chances to get a decent car. So he bought me a 1993 Dodge Shadow, 2-door, AC and clean...and it was all mine! It may have been a used car, but it was brand new to me. I was the first one of my friends to get a car.

With the car, my father laid down some more rules. In the house by eleven on school nights, twelve-thirty on weekends, plus spend my allowance on gas. I'd never been good with saving money, so I panicked until my mother decided she would secretly help me by slipping me a few extra dollars.

Owning a car almost made me feel like an adult, and I enjoyed fantasizing about approaching adulthood until I returned to school after the Christmas and New Year's holidays. My guidance counselor waited until the last semester of senior year to tell me that I was short five credits.

In the ninth grade, I failed a Child Care class. Since I didn't take another elective class to make up for it, I had to find something now or I could not graduate with my class. Fortunately the last period of the day was free for me, so having space in my schedule wasn't the problem; finding a suitable elective was. It turned out that the classes I had an interest in didn't have any seats available, so I ended up right back in the class I dreaded and failed: Child Care. I took the form filled out by my guidance counselor and I dragged along to the last period of the day, barely making it to my seat when the late bell rang.

As soon as the late bell rang, as if on cue, our teacher, Mr. Hill, stood up from behind his desk to begin class. Mr. Hill was so cool, and he was definitely looking all that. He looked like he'd just graduated college, had a low haircut and waves, nice Dockers and shirt. Seeing him made me think that my thoughts of this class being a breeze was confirmed, but it didn't take me long to realize that I'd thought wrong. That is, he was all right with me until he put me and Gary Simmons together. I was heated! I had done a good job of avoiding Gary so I wouldn't have to deal with him, and Mr. Hill hands me right over to him. I didn't know how I would get through this semester being Gary's "wife" without strangling him.

I didn't know Gary personally. At first I couldn't stand him because whenever I would see him around school, he was cutting back or busting on someone, playing the dozens. It was always, "your momma is so fat..." or somebody's last year's sneakers. Some of his jokes were funny, but I did my best to avoid him, especially since it seemed the whole school knew about Sasha.

When Gary heard Mr. Hill say he was pairing him up with me, the first question out of his mouth was "so do we have to do sissy stuff?"

Mr. Hill went on to explain that we were to pretend we are actually married, working out a budget according to our home life situations, children, and anything else that was thrown in the mix. There were a lot of groans and moans from all of the students, but those weren't going to help us get through this semester.

"I wanted to cruise through this class to get my credits for graduation," Gary said, wiping his hand over the top of his head a few times while leaning back in his chair.

I was there for the same reason, but it was obvious that we would not cruise through here. With Gary as my partner, I seriously questioned if we would get at least a C. By the end of class, Mr. Hill gave us our outlined assignments for the semester. It seemed like I had the most work for that class than any other.

Speaking to Gary after class, we agreed to begin our assignment that night at my house. When I got home and told my mother about the class, my complaints and Gary's visit that evening to start on our project. My mother told me to, "Make sure that den is straightened up before the young man gets here." So right after dinner I put my father's slippers beside his chair, dusted the coffee table, and moved the old newspapers stacked beside my father's chair to the kitchen to be bundled. Then I turned on the television, flipping through the channels for something to watch until Gary arrived. At seven o'clock on the dot, the doorbell rang and I found Gary standing there appearing to be ready to work with a pencil tucked behind his left ear, and his right hand in his pocket.

After introducing Gary to my parents, we went to the den to begin our assignment. I was disappointed when Gary only had input when he didn't agree with a decision I made. Everything he had to say was so critical unless it was his suggestion, and by the time he was ready to go, I was ready to strangle him. The easiest part about working with Gary was agreeing on what time to meet at my house that night.

"We're finished for tonight. When we meet again, you should have researched the car information you need, as well as your employment situation," I said, putting my notebook into my book bag.

"Yeah, yeah, whatever. I figure you could do all that since you got the notes. I got other things to do," Gary said, putting his pencil behind his ear and folding his hands behind his head.

"Whatever! Look, I am *not* doing my work and your work too," I said, becoming totally frustrated with Gary.

"Okay bet, I'll get all this info so you can stop crying. We still have to figure in the kids," Gary said, winking a hazel eye at me.

As much as Gary was getting on my nerves, I was beginning to really like looking into his eyes. He had eyelashes longer than any guy I had ever seen, and he wore his hair in a fancy cornbraid style. Just like most guys our age, he sagged his jeans, but not very far from his waist. Gary wore his Timberlands with the laces untied, but they somehow looked neat, and he was wearing a nice plaid shirt to match his jeans. He wasn't very muscular, but he was definitely looking better than he did in class that day.

"Well look, I'mma be out, alright? Just let me know when you want to meet again," Gary said, getting to his feet and stretching as if he worked just as hard as I did.

"A week from today is cool," I suggested, turning away from his hypnotic gaze.

"Alright then," Gary said, shifting the pencil behind his ear.

I walked Gary to the door and was about to close it when he turned around.

"Tonya, you're all right, you know that?" Gary said, smiling almost as if he were embarrassed to tell me that.

"Yeah, right" was the only thing I could think of to say because I sure didn't believe him.

"No, I'm straight up. Maybe we really can work a kid into this *marriage* thing. Maybe even two," said Gary, reaching out with his hand to stroke my cheek.

"Whatever. You just better have your business straight when we get together in a week," I said, pretending not to notice his touch.

"Why don't you come by my house for the next one? I'll serve some milk and cookies," he said, trying to smother a laugh.

"I'll think about it, Mr. Funny Guy."

"You do that," said Gary as he walked down the front stairs.

I closed the door and went back to the den to start on my other homework and put Gary Simmons as far out of my mind as possible. He was kind of cute though. Ok, really cute, but I decided it wouldn't be a good idea to get too close to him.

• • •

Gary and I made plans throughout the semester to get together and work on our project. One week we would meet at my house and then his, alternating weeks as we went along. One thing that surprised me about Gary was he really pushed to get our assignments in on time. He would check and then re-check our answers and information and made sure I agreed with what we put together. As much as Gary liked to joke, he was actually serious about making his grades.

The night we completed our assignment, I was at a point where I thought I would end up pulling my hair out. We were at Gary's house arguing about the finishing touches, just like we did for the whole semester. Usually I would stand my ground and stick with my choices until I was convinced Gary's suggestion was better than mine. Nothing came easy with Gary, and he made me explain why I chose to do certain things. To keep the arguing to a minimum, I just agreed with everything that he said so I could head home.

Just as we closed our notebooks, Gary's mother walked into the kitchen through the back door carrying groceries. She always entered a room like a whirlwind brought her in, but she was a pretty nice person. A petite lady with a short and naturally curly hair-do, Mrs. Simmons seemed to be in a hurry all the time, rushing to do one thing in order to do another. Usually that meant she had to rush home to do something so she can run back out to see a friend or take care of something else.

"Hello, Tonya, how are you? Gary, get the rest of the bags out of the car for me, will you please?" Mrs. Simmons said placing the bags she had in her hand on the counter top.

"Would you like for me to help?" I still didn't feel real comfortable around Gary's mother because it seemed like she was as young as we were. My mother's about her age and never acted this way, so it seemed a little weird to me. Gary's mother asked questions about girls or told him things about her friends or someone she met while she was out, and where she would be going as if Gary were her brother and not her son. That *never* happened with my parents

"Oh, no, that's ok. Gary can handle it. How is the project going?" she asked, opening the refrigerator to put the milk in it.

"We just finished it, thank God."

"That's good," Mrs. Simmons said, still giving the groceries her attention.

Gary came back in and that ended my conversation with his mother until I said good night. It was eight-thirty and I was starving since I decided to just grab a snack before I left home to go to Gary's house.

As Gary walked me to my car he suggested that we grab a burger at the local diner near the edge of town. As usual I had to call my parents to get permission. Once I got the okay from my mother, we headed across town in my car to the diner. Although we were not on an official date, I felt like I had to watch my table manners and wipe my mouth after every bite of my burger.

Gary's a sweet guy and though I didn't want to admit it, I kinda liked him. His medium build and that pretty, smooth skin and all! He must have gotten his eyes from his father because his mother's eyes are dark. We talked for a long time, even after we were through eating. I can't remember ever enjoying myself this much with a guy before. Maybe it's because I had never really been out on a date before. Besides it was a good change in comparison to James who was aggressive and demanding. Gary gave me a chance to express myself and he really listened to what I had to say. I could tell by the comments he would make, or the answers he gave when I asked a question.

"So what are your plans after graduation?" Gary wanted to know, changing the subject to school and our favorite subject.

"I want to sing, but my parents told me to start looking into school or other career opportunities," I said, waving my hand dismissing that idea.

"I didn't know you sing for real. I thought you just said that for the project. Where do you sing?"

"In church only," I answered, unable to keep the smile off my face.

"I want to hear you."

"What? No, I don't sing to just one person…"

Gary and I went back and forth with this silly thing, finally deciding that he'd sing with a recorded song, for help. I would sing without any help since I was the "songstress." Suddenly feeling up to the challenge, I agreed. After Gary paid the check, insisting I keep my money, we raced to my car like little kids. We fished through the tapes to find something he wanted to sing. Why did he choose my Earth, Wind and Fire tape? Of all the songs, he chose to sing "Reasons." Voice cracking, face contorted and frowning, he hit the worst falsetto note I'd ever heard. While he sang, I thought that he needed to take more than a few singing lessons. "Reasons…the reasons that we're here; the reasons that we're here…"

humming the words he didn't know. I was barely able to hold my laughter. Then the song ended.

"What are you laughing at? You know I could blow Phillip Bailey up any day," Gary said, sitting back in his seat smiling, trying not to laugh.

"Yeah right, in between the cracks in your voice," I said, laughing again as a few tears rolled down my cheeks.

Laughing, Gary asked, "So who got jokes now? We'll see who will be laughing last and the hardest. Come on, let's see what you can do, *Whitney Houston*...or should I call you *Janet Jackson?*"

"Whatever, Phillip Bailey wannabe...just give me time to choose a song."

I tried to think of something simple and quick and I finally decided on a church song about a man beside a highway begging. I closed my eyes, tuned Gary out and saw myself singing before our congregation. When I finished, there was nothing but silence.

"Well?" I asked, beginning to feel a little uncomfortable.

"Girl, you can blow like that? Why didn't you tell me before?" Gary asked, appearing to be completely blown away.

"It never came up. Besides, I only sing for our church choir."

"All jokes aside, Tonya, you can sing to me any time," Gary said, stroking my cheek with his fingertips.

Gary's touch caused me to feel something new so pulling away from him, I told him that we should head home. Before something actually happened, I thought to myself, not wanting to say those words aloud to Gary. It was getting very close to my curfew and I didn't want to hear my father's lecture, so I hurried and dropped Gary off at his house then drove home as fast as I could. Once I made it to my room, I let go of the breath I didn't know I was holding. Just as I turned the doorknob, my father called out from his room, "Good night, Tonya..." I knew it was his way of letting me know that he knew that I just made it in before curfew, so I quickly said "good night" to both of my parents and started preparing for bed.

As soon as my head hit the pillow, my evening with Gary filled my thoughts. That night I started seriously thinking about Gary. I found him to be a very sensitive, caring person. He looked good and all, and he had something I never knew a guy could have since most times my friends and I called them dogs. Maybe what we said was wrong and there really are a few good guys. I wondered if I was willing to find out or if Gary was the one to take that chance with.

The hard work, time and commitment for the Child Care Class paid off because our presentation was excellent! Mr. Hill was just as impressed as our classmates. We were able to stay within our budget, save a little money, take care of our household bills and two children too. For all of our hard work, we were rewarded an "*A.*" When Mr. Hill announced our grade to the class, Gary still had jokes, saying it worked out because he was the man of the house and he ran things. I didn't care what he said. Just real happy we made our grade.

As soon as the bell rang, dismissing our class and school for the day, classroom doors opened and boisterous students filled the halls. I headed towards the classroom door to join them when I felt Gary's hand on my left shoulder. He asked me out to the movies to celebrate that coming Saturday night. I agreed since I wanted to get to know him a little better. I knew I couldn't tell my parents the real reason I wanted to go out with Gary. In light of Sasha's condition and my father's words concerning it, I started to try and come up with something creative and convincing, but then realized my best bet was to tell the truth and deal with what my parents would say.

I wasn't surprised that my mother said it was fine. She said an "*A*" was worth celebrating and had no problem with me going to see a movie with Gary. My father said that Gary could come over for dinner on Sunday to celebrate until my mother told him we were just going to the movies.

The movie was all right, but since Gary was low on cash, we had to go to the cheap movie and catch an old flick. He refused to allow me to pay my own way, talking about chivalry ain't dead. So I let it live that night and saw *A Low Down Dirty Shame*, something we could have watched on TV. So much for chivalry when Gary was a little short on cash and the only movie he could afford that weekend was at the cheap movie theater that showed old movies for three dollars. I was all right with it though since it gave me an opportunity to do something other than homework with Gary.

After the movie, Gary drove around a little and then parked at *The Hill*. The Hill was a popular place at the far end of the park that separates our town from the next town. Mostly teen-agers and college students hang out there to get their groove on. I've heard about the crazy things that happen up there, so I was a little uncomfortable when Gary mentioned going there. There were already two other cars parked when we arrived, but Gary said more would come the later it got. According to him, ten o'clock at night was still pretty early on a Saturday night.

Looking to my right I began to follow the trees, tracing them all the way to my left. They seemed to have been planted to purposely create a semi-private atmosphere. There were no street lights and the darkness that surrounded us felt like I could reach out and touch it. But when I looked up at the sky, it was so clear with countless stars, a half moon and a few clouds that drifted by for a backdrop, making the night have a mystical feel to it. I sighed, sat back in my seat and tried to feel better about being up at The Hill.

"You alright?" Gary asked, pushing my hair out of my face.

"Yeah, I'm cool," I lied.

"If you're not feelin' this, we can go. I didn't bring you up here to try anything," Gary said, taking my hand.

"No, I'm straight."

To help put me at ease, Gary started talking about our project and the grade we made together. Our project evoked some serious thoughts of marriage and family life that I'd never considered. If I went by looks, having children with Gary would be a plus. Finding out that he's good with finances and other types of planning for the home only added to the possibilities of choosing him for a mate.

Gary said our project came easy for him because he helps his mother a lot around the house with repairs, and sometimes with their budget. His parents were divorced and his relationship with his father strained, something that is the force behind him working hard to learn how to take care of a family.

"I didn't know you had so much responsibility at home. Is your father still alive?" I wanted to know.

"Yeah, he's still living. But ever since he divorced my moms and re-married, I'm not a real part of his new life and family. What kind of father is that?" Gary said, turning to stare out of his window.

"How do you know he feels that way? Did you even..." I tried to say before Gary cut me off.

"I heard him telling my mother. I heard him say the words," Gary said, turning back to me, his voice just above a whisper. "That's the day that I promised myself I would stay away from him until I am old enough to tell him how much of a punk he really is."

Gary and I both fell silent. We just sat there holding hands until I noticed that it was time for me to go home. There was no way I wanted to end up on punishment the first time I actually went out on a real date. I liked Gary a lot, but he was not worth getting on a week's punishment for, so I told him that we should start to head back home.

"Yeah alright. I hope you had a good time with me tonight," Gary said, pushing my hair away from my face again.

"Yeah, I did," I answered, smiling at Gary.

"Can I kiss you then?"

Before I could answer, Gary pulled me to him and kissed me real sweet on my lips. My stomach fluttered and a nice, warm feeling started from my stomach, traveling to my cheeks. Even though it felt good, I was afraid and a little excited at the same time. And I believe my heart started beating a little quicker. After the kiss, butterflies were marching to music of their own accord in my stomach! I had a sudden urge to kiss Gary again, but second thoughts of him thinking I was hot squelched that idea.

Gary started the engine and headed back towards my house. Taking my fingers up to his lips, Gary kissed them and placed my hand back in my lap as he guided his car down the path towards the main street. Once we were on the main street, Gary took my hand in his again, bringing them to his lips, kissing each finger tenderly. We rode through town, and it seemed to be quite a few couples walking, holding hands, and enjoying the warm spring night and each other. This only served as a backdrop that fueled my heightened emotions, making the urge for me to want to kiss Gary even stronger. That moment was the first time I felt I stopped being a girl and had stepped over into womanhood.

When Gary parked his car in front of my house, he took my hand and kissed the back of it before I went in. Funny his kissing my hand had the same effect as his kiss on my lips, or it might be that I was still feeling the effects of his kiss lingering on my lips.

When I went inside, my parents were sitting up in the den watching television, cuddling on the sofa while waiting for me to come home. They asked if I'd enjoyed myself, and then my mother reminded me to get my things ready for church the next day.

As I went upstairs to get my things ready for the next day, I overheard my parents say they really liked Gary. So do I. That was the first time I allowed myself to admit that. Before I got into bed, I turned on my computer and typed in the details of my night out with Gary in my journal. I got into bed shortly after I finished typing, but sleep was slow in coming while my thoughts were full of Gary, his pretty eyes, pretty skin and especially when I thought on that sweet, sweet kiss...

## Chapter Six

Nothing could have prepared me for the college experience; everything was brand new. Most of the people I met there seemed to be in their own world, doing their own things. This experience was a culture shock since the college I attended was a Christian college. Long hair, short hair, baldheads, crazy clothes, smoking and drinking were still a part of the college scene I thought I would be getting away from by attending a Christian college. I was grateful for the decision not to live on campus, although I don't believe I would have been too tempted to do drugs or drink. Most of the students involved in those things attended this school because they attended Christian or Catholic schools in grade school, or their parents want them to become more grounded.

Seeking the comfort of something or someone familiar, Denise and I began spending more time together. We would go out for pizza, to the movies or hang out at each other's homes. I had to get used to not having Lisa and Sasha here because they decided to go to school as far away from home as possible. It gave Denise and me an opportunity to learn things about each other that we wouldn't have known. Since she decided to become an Administrative Assistant, Denise didn't feel the need to attend a college or university since business schools were popping up in almost every town. Denise attended a local business school that opened a few years before we graduated high school in the area of town near the mall. It already had a good reputation for turning out qualified people who were able to meet the challenge of the workforce. They offered twelve-month and eighteen-month courses, and the price of tuition was far less than any college.

Things worked out fine since I stayed home as well. On days that Denise missed her bus, I would give her a ride to school until she was able to buy a car. Denise's career choice didn't surprise me because she had always loved to type and to organize things. Her career choice did not cause a conflict with her father as mine did with my parents.

Denise opened up more as we got to know her. One subject Denise refused to discuss was her mother. All we ever knew was that she didn't make the trek from Atlanta to New Jersey with the rest of the family. About a month into the first semester we were in my room trying to decide what we were going to do on a Saturday night when Denise decided to confide in me her true feelings about her mother. She didn't want anyone to know that her mother had found a new man and he didn't want her kids. Denise's brother came home from school one day and found a letter taped to the refrigerator from their mother saying she left and that she was sorry. That left Denise's father to finish raising them while their mother went off and started a new life without them. Her father was too crushed to stay in Atlanta, so he moved the family back to his home state of New Jersey, a place Denise had only visited in the past. Feeling totally unwanted by her mother, it wasn't very easy for her to trust anyone. The way Denise dressed and carried herself was a diversion to hide the embarrassment of not having her mother in the home. To be honest, it just made people think she was a geek or mental case.

I remember when we first started hanging out with Denise. She was a bit on the shy side, though she definitely had her moments when she would speak up. Of the four of us, she was the most reluctant to date, much less find interest in a guy. Whenever the rest of us would have something to say about guys, Denise didn't say much of anything. But when she did, it would cause us to think about what we said or attempted to do. She didn't base her choices on any particular belief, but stood on what was reasonable or made the most sense to her.

She didn't even consider dating until the summer after our junior year in high school. We were on one of our famous trips to the mall, doing a little window-shopping, and eating at the food court. The mall was the place to be if you were to be anywhere in our city. Even if we couldn't afford to buy the clothes that were in fashion, at least we knew what was in and copied it the best we could. Then there was the game room where all the high school guys hung out to play video games and meet girls. Next to the game room was a record store that sold the latest R&B, Gospel, Jazz, or whatever kind of music you wanted. We would spend at least an hour listening to music, mainly sampling for free. Most times we didn't buy anything, but we came away knowing most of the words to the new songs that were out. From there we would pretty much stroll through the mall and do people-watch. Mothers pushing baby carriages, little kids crying because they couldn't have something they wanted, couples holding hands and sharing ice cream, and the teens that traveled in groups doing much of the same things my friends and I did.

As we all walked towards Macy's, we heard someone calling Denise's name. Johnny Haines came walking towards us. He was six, eight, cornbraids, from the front to the back of his head, and a gold hoop earring in his left ear. His long legs brought him quickly to where we stood. After speaking to the rest of us, he took Denise aside to talk. Denise put both hands in her back pockets and seemed to be listening intently to Johnny, nodding her head a few times at his words.

When they finished, Denise hurried back to us, half-walking and half-skipping, bubbling over with excitement. All of a sudden her lack of interest in guys changed, and it was more than obvious Johnny had something to do with that. Covering her face with her hands, Denise almost shouted, "He asked me out, he asked me out! I can't believe Johnny Haines wants to go out with me...I just can't believe it!" The way I saw it, it was about time she dated somebody. Johnny was cute too, and was the star power forward of our school's varsity basketball team. I couldn't help wondering how he could see anything past Denise's big clothes.

Denise is almost as tall as Lisa, but skinny and shapely when her clothes didn't hide it. She wore her shoulder length hair in different curled styles and has the prettiest big eyes I've ever seen. She has a medium brown complexion with a few pimples that flared up every now and then, and that she didn't bother to do much about. With all I thought she had working against her, something was working right that day at the mall when the star basketball player asked her out.

We continued to browse through the stores and found a new store with trendy teen fashions. Denise spotted a white, sleeveless fitted summer dress with spaghetti straps to try on. We were all shocked, but Denise blew us off and headed for the dressing room. She was strong-willed at times, saying what is on her mind without holding back. Not mean or anything most times, but she will put it right on out there. When she came out of the dressing room, I had to admit it was a definite improvement over anything I've ever seen her wear.

"This is for my date with Johnny on Saturday. He's taking me to the concert in the park to hear a few bands. How do you think this looks?" Denise asked, turning to check her reflection at different angles.

"It's nice, Denise. Maybe you won't look so frumpy," said Lisa, nudging me in the ribs.

"Anyway, this dress is for Johnny. If he likes it, maybe I'll come back to this store and buy some more clothes," Denise said as she headed toward the dressing room, pulling the spaghetti strings from her shoulders before she disappeared behind the curtains.

Denise made her purchase and we caught the bus to go back home. We rode the bus home, talking about how Denise should act on her first date. We were laughing and carrying on so bad, several passengers repeatedly stared at us.

We spent the rest of the summer doing the same old things: the mall, hanging at each other's house and trying to come to grips with the fact that adulthood was closer than we realized, only we still had no idea what it entailed. We didn't have summer jobs because our parents didn't push the issue. Lisa still had to keep an eye on her younger brothers and sister occasionally, and Sasha made her mother feel guilty about her life and pretty much bribed her for money. My parents felt I should consider doing volunteer work so my high school career would look good on paper when I applied to colleges. Of course I didn't agree to this, but I had to volunteer down at the church with my mother at least once a week. There were specific days for certain ministries, and my mother was in charge of the feedings and clothing giveaways that took place every Wednesday at noon. I had to greet the people who came in and escort them to a seat at one of the tables. Next I would prepare a tray of food and serve them. My mother said it would teach me about humility and servitude, but all I could remember is being bored for two whole hours.

That summer Denise was absent from our foursome, her first date with Johnny was just the beginning of the changes we would see in her other than her clothing. Instead of hanging out with us, she would be with Johnny, even if it was just to go down to the courts to watch him play basketball. She didn't mind walking down the street holding hands or allowing Johnny to hug her and even kiss her in public! In the past

Denise would have a fit whenever we would see couples displaying affection in public. She wore her curls out most of the time, and bought clothes that were fitting. Denise's relationship had her so occupied that we hardly saw her that whole summer.

During our senior year in high school, Denise and Johnny were inseparable. By the time we were freshman in college, Denise's relationship with Johnny changed a little. Since he was away at college, Denise and I spent every spare moment together, including weekends. We would vent about our problems concerning guys, our favorite topic. We talked about what we would do once we finished college and secured employment, and what was most important to us in life and a host of other personal thoughts we had not shared with anyone else.

But by the time the second semester of our freshman year rolled around, Denise started canceling simple plans like going to the movies on a Saturday, or special events like our trip into New York. It wouldn't have bothered me so much if Lisa and Sasha were going to be home for Thanksgiving. They were even thinking about staying in Cali for the Christmas holiday and Winter Break. Since Denise was canceling plans with me, I thought everything between Johnny and her had changed for the better.

The last time Denise pulled her disappearing act, no one said anything, but this time I was. We had really started sharing things and getting to know each other better and here she is tripping over a guy! Aside from feeling a little slighted by Denise's absence, I wanted to know just what was going on with her and Johnny. As I walked to Denise's house, I thought about just forgetting the whole thing, but curiosity got the best of me and I made the short walk down the street to Denise's house. Denise answered the door when I rang the doorbell.

"Hey, Tonya, what's up? Come on in...I'm watching TV in the living room."

The Warren household looked almost as weird as the way Denise used to dress. The big beige sofa and loveseat didn't fit properly in the small living room, neither did her father's lumpy looking, worn-out easy chair. When I walked through the door, Mr. Warren was sitting in his chair reading his newspaper. He was an average-sized man, about five-ten, one hundred-seventy pounds, and never said much. He had a small, neat afro with a broad nose, wide mouth and uneven, discolored teeth. As usual, he got up and excused himself to give Denise and me some privacy.

"Denise, I came over to see how you were doing, and...well, I haven't heard a word from you in about a week. What's going on?" I sat on the sofa.

"Oh, you know, just been visiting Johnny at his campus. I can't stand going so many days without spending time with him," she said as if it were no big deal.

"You go there every weekend? I mean, I'm not trying to be all up in your business, but you hardly let Johnny breathe."

"Something wrong with that?" Denise asked, suddenly becoming defensive.

"No, but you don't even call or hook up with me anymore. I felt like we were getting closer, you know?"

"I've been spending all my free time with Johnny, that's why. I really think I love him, Tonya."

"Haven't you and Johnny built up a level of trust in your relationship so that you don't have to go check on him every week? What is the real deal, Denise?"

"It's not that I don't trust Johnny, it's the girls at his school. Since he's a basketball star, they're all on his tip, even when I'm there! I want them to know that he's taken, but some of them don't even care, they will just walk up and start talking to Johnny as if I wasn't there."

I felt sorry for her, I really did, but what could she possibly do? I wanted to tell her to leave Johnny alone because it's going to be about basketball and girls for now, and she may lose him because of it, but I didn't have the heart to say it. Instead I asked her why she didn't think about transferring to the same college so that she could at least keep up with Johnny and her grades. From what she said, her grades were slipping and she almost flunked out of school.

"Are you kidding me? I couldn't get into that college if I stayed over night on the front steps of the school. It's too expensive. My father can't afford it, and now my grades are too jacked up to even try for a scholarship of any kind. Besides, I have something working for me that will keep Johnny in my life forever," Denise said with a hint of a frown on her face. "I'm having his baby, but Johnny wants me to get an abortion."

"You're…pregnant? Denise, how could you let yourself get into a situation like this? How could you?"

"Shhh, Tonya! If my father finds out, he'll trip. I'm not ready to tell anyone else because with Johnny denying that he is the father, there's going to be more than enough drama when the baby is born. I know he's saying that to make me get rid of it, but I'm not going to do that."

All kinds of emotions hit me, one behind the other:…shock, amazement, disbelief, shame, disgust, empathy. The last thing I would ever do was to advise Denise on what she should do about her pregnancy, but the decisions she had been making lately had totally changed any respect I had for her. Her knack for making sound judgment was all gone because of a guy. I realized Denise was probably confused because she never had a boyfriend before Johnny. I tried to give Denise the benefit of the doubt instead of judging her.

• • •

Brown/Stamford College was a seventy-five year old Christian College that boasted not only academics; their theology department was known for the highly respected and renowned religious leaders who had earned their degrees in their hallowed halls. The campus sat on two and a half acres of land. Old bricks covered in lush ivy in the spring and summer. The walkways were cobblestone, and led to the different buildings that were located on the site according to the subjects being taught. The classrooms varied in size and content. The auditorium had a place of its own on the campus. It was built away from the academic buildings, and surrounded by a cleared field for outdoor concerts. To be honest, I wasn't sold on going to the college until I saw the auditorium. It was there I could visualize myself on stage belting out a song that I'd just written. It also reminded me of the time my friends and I decided to put together a group of our own. It didn't last long, but we had fun with it the day Sasha suggested we sing together. We had gotten together our own rendition of *His Eye Is On The Sparrow*. Talk about singing! We were kickin' it like that when we looked up and saw my mother standing in the door. One by one we stopped singing.

We all tried our best to protest, telling my mother it was for fun, but she didn't even care, she just continued to set up the tape player and gave us our cue to sing the song again and we did as if we were auditioning for a recording contract. When we finished, Mom stopped the tape, rewound it and played it back so we could hear ourselves. She was acting like she had just discovered us. We all had to admit our singing was tight. Denise just needed to sing out a little more, but otherwise we were all right. That was when I knew for sure that I wanted to make singing a career.

Attending Brown/Stamford College was my one-way ticket to my lifelong dream.

During sophomore year, I became more focused on my goal of singing professionally. In order to achieve my goals and please my parents at the same time, I threw myself into my studies, cutting out any extracurricular things like hanging out with Denise or anything else that didn't have anything to do with music or singing. It wasn't long before Denise got the hint and stopped asking me to hang out.

My life was totally about school and church, and definitely in that order.

I still had not declared my major, but carried a full load of required courses, including a few electives in music education. I learned a lot about the history of music and the flavor different cultures gave to it. That heightened my desire to make music my life. I was consumed with music yet I was able to maintain a 3.5 g.p.a. The stress from the lack of sleep and countless hours in seclusion definitely had me wound up. There were a few times I went overboard in the way I spoke to my parents and friends. I would be brief and sometimes a little rude, having to go back later to apologize. No matter how hard it was with the pressure from classes, the school choir and my own church choir had become my life, there was no way I wanted to give up anything. I just kept seeking ways to add on to it, convinced that all of my hard work would pay off soon.

I opted to take a class to learn how to read and write music during the summer semester. I had toyed around with writing a few songs and felt that if I could read the notes and write my own lyrics, it could only be a plus for my career. My parents assumed I was doing it to help the choir out, and I said nothing to change their thoughts. I figured I could use what I learned in the class to put music to the few songs I'd written years before and write some new ones to present to the choir when school started in the fall. I usually stayed close to home, except for a movie or to the mall by myself.

One surefire way to flex my vocals and with my parents approval was by joining the college choir. The choir was as awesome as I'd heard. Since it was a choir, my parents did not object when I joined at the end of my freshman year.

The last part of my stroll to becoming a professional singer was joining the semi-professional singing group called *The Inspirations*. We didn't make a lot of money, but I enjoyed the experience of riding from town to town, singing in auditoriums at other colleges or concert halls.

My singing career had become my main focus, but not without constantly bumping heads with my parents, especially my mother. She insisted that I declare my major in my sophomore year, so to appease her, I began taking some Early Childhood Education classes to see if it was something I liked. But I continued to minor in music and take as many classes as I could. My mother didn't mind the choir, but it was a fight to the finish my entire sophomore year to finally get her to allow me to sing with *The Inspirations*. That's why it took me so long to join. It depended on my being able to juggle class work, choir and church obligations. Her argument was that I could not possibly handle a full load of classes, the choir at school and at church as well as any other obligations without something going lacking. I didn't give up trying to convince my mother, finally understanding why the widow woman in the Bible kept going before the unjust judge to help her, which he eventually did after growing weary of the woman's constant requests. Only I felt my mother had wronged me and was the unjust judge at the same time in my case. All of the work for my classes had to be completed and handed in on time; grades no lower than a "B", no excuses. I still had to sing in the choir at my church and find a way to attend any rehearsals we had unless my absence was related to academics, and I still had to give a little time to the Youth Department.

Somehow I was able to juggle all these things and still have time to enjoy singing with *The Inspirations*. I'd become fast friends with the other two female singers and the two guys, the drummer and keyboard player; but we never did anything outside the group. Sam, who was the only male lead singer, was very easy to talk to, and I often found myself staying a little longer after rehearsal to vent my frustrations about school and parents. Sam would listen and share some of his own stories to help keep me encouraged. Sam told me from the time I first joined the group to consider it as a family, and he was the big brother. He was very understanding when I started having problems with my car, becoming frustrated when I ran in at the last minute, but he would apologize later.

The girls in the group would tell me not to take Sam's attitude personally or seriously because he was a perfectionist with the heart of a teddy bear. The guys would just say it was part of being involved with the whole music scene and like the family we were, there was bound to be a little tension from time to time. I figured they knew what they were talking about since they'd been in the group for a while.

Sam formed the group the first semester of his freshman year in his dorm room starting with Jackie, who sang first soprano. They dated during that first year and remained friends thereafter, but the way they argued sometimes, I thought something was still going on between them. Bobby, the keyboard player and Allen, the drummer, joined when the group was first formed. Liz, who sings high alto and second soprano, joined two years later. They would take advantage of good weather and sing right outside of Sam's dorm room and at different functions held locally until the popularity of the group caught on in a big way.

Although their words comforted me and proved to be true, I didn't fully accept their words until things blew over, usually after we finished a concert. Once we went out on that stage and the music started to play, all of my bad thoughts disappeared and I gave myself over to the feeling of total satisfaction that singing always gave to me.

But after a year of my lateness, I understood why Sam's frustration had turned into disappointment and anger.

Sam's disapproval was a bit harsher the day before Spring Break.


My car broke down on the highway on my way to school. I was already running late, and we were hosting a special Easter concert, but I knew I was in trouble when my car started smoking from under the hood

"Aw man! Now what?" I said out loud. I pulled my hoopty over to the side, the white smoke getting thicker and smelling like burning rubber. *What am I going to do now,* I thought.

I waited fifteen minutes and tried to start the car. All it did was cough. I got out and looked around. Cars were passing by, but no one stopped. I opened the hood then got back into the car, hoping that someone would stop when they saw a woman in distress. I kept thinking that the group was going to be mad at me again and I couldn't blame them.

Cars flew by, traveling much faster than the posted 55mph signs, causing my car to rock from side to side. I looked up at the sky and noticed the dark clouds and the threat of rain. I kept wishing someone would at least stop to make sure I was all right. Instead all I got was a rocking car while I watched the trees and store signs blow in the wind, the smell of the oncoming rain floating through my window.

Opening the hood hadn't made a difference either. I thought, *Where was a cop when you needed one?* Just as I got out of the car to put the hood down, a gray car with tinted windows all around pulled up behind mine. I was a little afraid because I didn't recognize the car so I got back into my car as fast as I could and locked my door. I immediately started busying myself with something on the passenger seat. Next thing I know, there's a knock at the window.

"Gary! I'm so glad it's you!" I rolled the window down.

"What's going on?"

"This car has been putting me down all semester. I'm late for a concert and I'll probably get kicked out of the group and..." I said quickly before Gary interrupted.

"Calm down and let me take a look and see if we can get you going" Gary helped me out of my car. "This is my man, Frank. Frank, this is Tonya."

Frank and I talked while Gary checked the car out. Frank told me they were traveling the other direction across the highway when Gary spotted my car.

"Who's been doing piece work up under here?" Gary asked, interrupting the conversation between Frank and myself.

"My father's fake mechanic. Why?"

"Call your father and have him tow this thing home. It's not going anywhere. All of these little minor fixes caused you a bigger problem, but not something that can't be fixed," Gary said, dropping the hood soundly.

"Man! How am I going to get to the concert? Even if I take a bus now, it'll be too late."

"What do you think, Frank? You got time to check out a concert?" Gary wiped his hands on his jeans.

"Yeah, why not? Where's the concert?"

"At my school, just fifteen minutes from here."

"Call your pops and have him tow your car and we're on our way," Frank said with a friendly smile while handing me his cell phone.

"Thanks, Frank. Excuse me a moment."

After talking with my father, I gathered my belongings and hopped in the back seat of Frank's car. It felt almost strange being in the same car with Gary because we had not spoken since this past Christmas. Our decision at that time was to remain friends, but neither of us bothered to stay in touch. I found myself watching how much I said to Gary, but I chattered away with Frank as if I had known him for years. I told him about the singing group and the choir, as well as the songs I had been writing. I told Frank about those things to indirectly let Gary know what I had been doing, hoping he would tell me what he had been up to. Gary just made a few comments while he pulled his dreads into a ponytail. They were so neat and clean that I had to lean up and smell them. Instead of smelling his hair, I got a whiff of his cologne. He smelled real good. Before I said something I would regret, I leaned back in my seat and continued to direct most of my conversation toward Frank.

When we arrived at the school, I gathered my things from the backseat and ran backstage to change.

"Tonya, you're late again! Do you want to be part of this group or what?" I had barely walked in and Sam was already at me.

"Sam, I'm sorry. My car broke down again and I finally got a ride and..."

"Save it! Go change, we're on next," Sam said, shooting daggers at me with his eyes.

I ran to the ladies room, freshened and changed and made it just in time to hear our name being called.

"Come on and give a hand for *The Inspirations*! Come on. Give it up! One of our own, ladies and gentlemen, right here at Brown/Stamford College, *The Inspirations*!"

I had just taken my place in front of the mike in front of the instruments a second before the curtain went back. The crowd went wild, calling our names and cheering until the first note and we began to sing. It looked like the whole audience was on their feet. I just closed my eyes and sang with my whole heart.

We began with some slow worship and praise songs as a way to encourage the audience to join us and feel our flow as we added our own modulations, twists, turns and riffs to a few of the old hymns. Then we started singing the first of what would be three new upbeat contemporary gospel songs that our keyboard player had written, adding a little rap in one song and a steady drum beat that felt like it thumped in time to the beat of my heart. As I looked over the crowd, I saw people jammin' and dancing to our music and getting into the lyrics of the song. I felt that we could make it on the top 10 of the R&B chart, it sounded so good.

As always, we finished with our own rendition of *Jesus Loves Me*. Everyone joined in and it was beautiful.

Once we were through singing our last song, Sam introduced us by name and what we did in the group. Since Sam did this at the end of every concert we did, a lot of the students knew who I was by name when they saw me. After the final bow, I hurried to the ladies room to change out of my sweat soaked clothes into some dry ones and set out to look for Gary and Frank. I figured they might have gone outside, so I headed for the door. The closer I got to the door, the more it sounded like someone arguing.

I rounded the corner and I could hear Gary's voice loud and clear. "She's with me. Simple as that."

"Never seen you around here before, man," I heard Sam say. "According to that college sweatshirt you have on, you're from the west coast."

"I don't owe you an explanation as to why I'm here. Frank, let's find Tonya so we can step."

"Sam, Gary, what's wrong?"

"This guy says he's with you," Sam said, one eye narrowed at Gary.

"He is. What's the problem?"

"I was looking out for you," Sam said, but he didn't sound too much like a friend.

"Are you ready to go, Gary?" I asked, turning away from Sam.

"You really know this guy, Tonya?" Sam stuffed both hands in his pockets.

"Yes, Sam, I do. He's one of my best friends. See 'ya after Spring Break," I said, dismissing the whole matter.

"Don't forget, Tonya, we have rehearsal our first night back," Sam said, still not looking or sounding too pleased.

"Yeah, yeah, I'll be there," I said.

I was glad when we made it to Frank's car. I was so exhausted that I lay down on the back seat.

"You alright back there?" Gary asked.

"I'm straight, just a little tired."

"Your group was kickin' it tonight, but what's up with your friend?"

"Sam? I don't know."

"Maybe he likes you," said Frank.

I don't know how Frank arrived at that conclusion, and although I felt defensive, I didn't allow it to creep into my voice. I tried to make light of their encounter with Sam. "I don't like him. Sam is just a guy in the group and our leader. He's all right once you get to know him."

We stopped off for a bite to eat at Wendy's. When Frank parked his car in front of my house, I thanked him and Gary for being there for me. I hurried to the front door and I let myself in, closing and locking the door behind me. I couldn't help thinking about Sam and his reaction to me today, especially after he met up with Gary. I didn't know who he might think Gary was to me, so I felt a slight obligation to be sure to tell him my first day back.

• • •

Normally after a concert, I would be totally exhausted. When Frank dropped me off, my parents weren't home, so I took the opportunity to run a nice, warm bubble bath. I soaked in the tub until the bubbles faded and the water turned cool, turning over thoughts of the concert, meeting Frank and trying to figure out Gary's standoffish attitude. By the time I had returned to my room, the phone rang. Before I could say "hello", Gary was saying, "What are you doing?"

At first I pretended like I didn't want to talk to him, but I missed him too much to keep pretending. But since it was getting late and I wasn't sure what time my parents would be home, I told him we could get together the next day. That's what we did...then and all the days during Spring Break.

The last night of the break started out as a double date with Frank and his girlfriend, Pat. She was cool, and we hit it off. At night's end, Frank left with Pat, and Gary and I drove up to The Hill in his car. Most days we were together, Gary was usually quiet. At first, I thought it was his way of showing that he was maturing. But I eventually came to notice that he was quiet with me and talked a lot around his friends and other people. He wouldn't allow his feelings to show on his face, so when we parked at The Hill, I didn't know what to expect from him. Gary turned off the car and pulled me closer to him and wrapped his right hand around my shoulder and stroked my cheek with his fingertips. This is the most intimate thing he had done during Spring break. Then he took his free hand, reached into his pocket and pulled something out, hiding it so I couldn't see.

"What's that?" I asked while trying to pry his hand open.

"Stop struggling and hold your hand out and you'll see. You won't see if you keep trying to get it from me," Gary laughed, pulling his hand away and out of my reach.

"Okay, okay, here's my hand...give it up."

Gary took my hand and placed a ring made with my initials and my birthstone under the "T." The ring fitted perfectly, and before I hugged Gary and thanked him, I clicked on the interior light of the car to get a better look.

"How did you know my size?"

"I took your old ring off that night you dozed off while watching movies at my house and had the size checked." Gary pulled my old ring from his pocket. I just smiled. It was such a sweet gesture. After I kissed Gary on his cheek, I thought about this token and asked Gary why he did it and he said because he wanted a committed relationship with me. Well, his exact words were that he "wanted me."

"You want me? Just like that? So this ring means more than you said?" I asked, automatically fingering the ring on my hand.

"No, it's a symbol of our friendship. I'm thinking about making things permanent though," Gary said, like he was running things, including me.

*102*

I had to set him straight right then and there on more than a few things. I was focusing on my singing career and nothing else, not even a relationship with him was going to change that. We constantly played a game of seesaw with each other; first I would be all into him and wanting him while he pulled back, and then it would be the other way around. This time I refused to allow myself to fall victim to the emotions that ruled my decisions whenever I dealt with Gary. He wasn't too happy about it. No matter what I said, he tried to come one better and discount my reasoning for not wanting anything more than friendship with him. He couldn't get that times had changed and people changed, that I was becoming a self-assured adult.

"Tonya, you're not making this easy," Gary said, turning my hand loose as if he had just realized he was still holding it.

"But I know what's right for me, and I have to make that choice. Understand?"

"I still don't get it, Tonya. You're not being fair. If I love you, I can't have you now. And if I look somewhere else, I'm wrong. You've got to make up your mind."

"If you love me like you say, you will wait for what we have to come together. If you just want to get some, you'll look somewhere else. Simple as that," I concluded.

"Whatever. I guess we have to wait and see where we go from here," Gary said, ending our conversation. He started the car and we rode to my house in silence. Before I went in the house, he told me he would only wait for my answer until the end of school, after that he would go on about his business. The last thing I heard were his tires screeching off into the night.

As I prepared for bed that night, I could still picture Gary's disappointed face and hear the sadness in his voice when he realized that things would not work out between us the way he wanted. But it didn't take long for thoughts of Sam to surface, overcrowding any thoughts of Gary. I had to think about how I would explain my relationship with Gary and apologize for being late all those times. Since I wanted to sing professionally, now was the time to prepare myself for it by being responsible and changing my level of commitment to the group. I was still having a hard time convincing my parents that singing professionally was something I could do and be successful at, without having to starve. This was still an ongoing battle in my house even after my parents came to see the group perform three times since I joined.

The desire to sing convinced me to make peace with Sam so I wouldn't blow my chances.

After classes the first day back, I hurried to the auditorium for practice. I figured I would be on time to prove that I'm going to try to do better. Instead of our normal rehearsal, we had a hard session with Sam barking orders at everybody, especially me. I knew it was because of what happened between him and Gary. When he continued to be mean, I decided that I wasn't explaining anything to him about Gary and me. The barking continued all through rehearsal, and I'd had just about enough of Sam, when he shouted, "Come on, Tonya, that's not the note! Take it from the top everybody." We started singing, and as soon as I came in, Sam stopped the song again. "Tonya, what have you been doing during Spring Break? If you spent more time singing instead of humping, you would get the note right."

"Who do you think you're talking to? Humping? Please!" I was angry and embarrassed by Sam's remarks.

"Yeah, you and that punk you brought here. Let's start all over. Kirk, maybe you should bring that note down one since Tonya's having a hard time getting it."

"The note is wrong and you know it, Sam. Why are you busting on me?"

"Let's go, we don't have all night. From the top!" He ignored me.

We sang the song all the way through this time without Sam bugging. After we finished out with prayer, everyone went home. I began to put my belongings in my backpack and started for the door.

"Tonya, what happened tonight?" Sam asked, standing in front of me with his arms folded.

"You know full well nothing happened, Sam," I said, letting him know I was angry with him.

"Maybe we need to replace you if you can't sing the songs right."

"Replace me? If it's all that, I can quit!" I was ready to square off with Sam.

"Don't make such a hasty decision. I guess I could let you hang around a little longer if you do as you're told," Sam rubbed under his nose a few times with his hand.

"Oh, you think you're my father or something?" I asked, challenging Sam.

"No, but I know what's best for you." Sam walked closer to me.

"Look, I'm out. Maybe I won't come back." I said, getting a sunken feeling in the pit of my stomach. The feeling you get when you know something bad is about to happen.

"I told you, as long as you cooperate, you can stay in the group."

Sam was in my face now and he looked strange. Scary.

"Like I said, I'm out."

I turned to leave and Sam snatched my arm. He snapped. "Your boyfriend screw you?"

By now, he was all up in my face.

"What? He's not my boyfriend!"

"Just giving him some, huh?"

"You're crazy! Get your hands off me!"

"Why don't you let me have a little? You don't seem to mind giving it to just anybody."

Sam grabbed both of my arms and held them down to my sides while he blew his hot breath in my face hard, making me look directly into his eyes. I finally found my voice and some strength and tried to work my way out of Sam's grip. Pushing Sam in his chest with both hands as hard as I could, I screamed, "No!!! Get off me, get your hands off me!!!"

I started screaming and struggling to get away from him. I thought about where I was, and the fact that no one comes to the auditorium unless something was going on. I kept screaming any way and praying that the Lord would send someone my way.

Sam screamed in my face. "Shut up, Tonya, shut up! Everybody went home. No one to rescue you so shut up and do what I say!"

"Get off me, get off me! Please...turn me loose!"

"Since it's obvious that you've been disobedient, it's up to me as the leader of this group to set you straight," Sam held me even tighter.

I screamed until Sam slapped me real hard across my face. I fell on the floor and he picked me up by my hair, dragging me causing my stockings to rip away from my legs.

"I told you to shut up! Now I'm really going to have to punish you. You're still being disobedient!" Sam screamed in my face.

"No, get off me! Please stop! Let me go!"

My constant screaming and begging didn't do anything but make Sam even angrier. He slapped me and kept on slapping me until the left side of my face felt numb. I didn't know what to do or say to make him stop. Then Sam grabbed me by my hair and made me look at him again. "This is a Christian group, Tonya, and there are certain rules we live by all the time. Now, do you understand what I'm saying?" He was calm, like he'd never laid a finger on me.

Somehow I got the strength to pull away and he slapped me again. I started screaming again so Sam punched me a couple times. I could feel that my face was bruised, and I could taste blood in my mouth. The tears ran down, but I couldn't muster up a real cry anymore. Sam pulled me up once more by my hair, but I couldn't stand because my legs were suddenly weak.

"Now let us go over the rules so you can stay in the group. Stand up!" His sneer sounded almost like a wild animal's growl. He grabbed my blouse, tearing it at the seam by my right arm. He took hold of the bottom of my skirt, raising it, digging his fingers hard into my thighs, lifting my skirt closer to my waist. I closed my eyes and braced myself for Sam to complete the violation of my body he had already started.

Then I heard the sound of a door opening. But then maybe I was just hearing things. Suddenly someone clicked the lights on, catching Sam off guard.

"Who...who is...?" stammered Sam.

"Who's in here?" the voice called out.

"It's Sam. I'm cleaning up and I'm getting ready to leave out. Who's that?" Sam said, totally composed, answering in a normal tone of voice.

"Jack Stevens. Security. Hurry up and finish in here so the doors can be locked."

"On my way."

"Help me, help me, help me!!!!" I screamed at the top of my lungs.

My face and mouth were bloody and I could hardly part my lips. All I knew was I had to scream in order to be rescued.

Jack Stevens walked behind the curtain, horrified at the scene before him. He immediately reacted, by pulling his nightstick, grabbing Sam in a headlock, and using his radio to get help. In one swift motion, Jack Stevens had everything under control, saving me from Sam.

"This is radio number five. I'm in the auditorium. I need emergency backup right now! Looks like an attempted rape in progress!" Officer Stevens struggled to keep Sam on the floor, telling him to hold still as not to get hurt. The police came and took Sam away in handcuffs. I lay on the cold floor, forcing myself to stay conscious. Blood ran from my mouth and my head pounded with pain that looked white behind my closed eyes. In all my wildest dreams, I never would have believed I could end up in a position like this, with my very life hanging in the balance. I felt unconsciousness overtaking me. I relinquished my will to it, welcoming the escape.

# Chapter Seven

Plans, decisions, aspirations, goals, and the things to do to achieve all that I'd ever dreamed of was literally smashed when Sam attacked me. The world I built for myself and the things I told myself to justify all of my decisions were gone, and I didn't have anything left inside to even begin to hope for a change in my life. How many times had I heard someone say that life wasn't fair, yet I couldn't identify because everything in my life was better than I could possibly ask for. The way I lived my life should have been enough to keep away danger, and the fact that I'd been in church all of my life should have protected me from what I'd experienced. Out of all of my friends, I was the one with the most stable home and parents who were always involved in my life whether I wanted them there or not. I had the curfews and the strict rules to live by, yet I turned out to be a failure.

Three months after my attack, I still found myself seeking solace and comfort in becoming a recluse. I figured if I didn't touch anyone, they couldn't touch me and I would never be hurt again. I stayed in the house watching so much television I could have created my own show. My bible remained inside the top drawer of my night stand instead of a part of my personal daily devotion time after I convinced myself there was nothing in there I needed. My mother got on my nerves hovering over me and trying to talk me into going shopping or somewhere else with her. As far as I was concerned, she was doing well to get me to go to church on Sunday. I couldn't hold my head any lower, and to continue going to church made absolutely no sense to me. The only ones at church who really knew what happened to me were my Pastor and his wife. I was too ashamed to share it with anyone else. I guess my Pastor thought he was helping when he would ask me to sing a solo, but I refused every time. I vowed I would never sing again, not in church or anywhere else. So to put an end to his requests for solos coming from me, I sat down with my Pastor in his office to discuss it.

I closed the door behind me when I went into his office because I wanted to hurry and say what I had to say and get it over with. Instead of staying calm and talking the way I had planned, I simply blurted out, "I'm not singing any more, Pastor, so please stop asking me."

"God has blessed you with a beautiful voice to sing His praises, Tonya," Pastor Jackson said as he patted my shoulder.

"I can't do it anymore. The desire is gone. I'm still wrestling with the incident. I haven't lived a shabby life, and I've always tried to do the right thing."

"Are you saved, Sweetheart?"

"Well, yes, but..."

"But you don't serve Him with all your heart. You come to church because that's all you've known your whole life. Your parents are saved and they brought you up in the fear and admonition of the Lord. Now you have to step out and learn of God for yourself, Tonya. You can't ride on your parents' salvation. You must know God for Tonya. He has a calling on your life that only you can yield to. There are no short cuts or ways around it. God has His hand in your life. Yield to Him, Daughter," Pastor said in a reassuring voice.

I didn't have anything to say after this, so Pastor prayed for me and I left. I just wanted to know why this had to happen to me, and after this meeting I was no closer to finding out than I was when I first went into the office. For a whole week after talking to Pastor, I moped around the house staying to myself as much as possible. This was the week Pastor Jackson had a guest evangelist at our church, so I was expected to be there every night with my parents. But the last thing I wanted to do was go to church on a Monday night, so I dragged along getting ready because I wanted my parents to leave me so I could be home alone. I thought my plan worked until I heard my mother call me. "Tonya, honey, are you ready to go?"

"I'm coming, Mom!" I hated the way my parents talked to me after the attack, as if they can't just say "Tonya, come on!" or "We're waiting on you!" like they usually would. Church at that? My father usually acted as if he was having a stroke if he was five minutes late. Fifteen minutes passed and he didn't say a word. It takes twenty minutes to get to church and my father didn't knock on my door once.

"Are you ready?" my father asked when I came downstairs.

"Yes, Dad, I'm ready. Had to fix this hair."

"Why don't you pin it up?" my mother suggested.

"Mom, please!" We rode to church in silence after that. It's not their fault that everything they say to me touches off a bad attitude lately. I mean, they've done all they could possibly do for me. It's just that I feel their controlling ways led to all that has happened to me. Everything was outlined, scheduled, with little flexibility. Curfews, the dos and the don'ts, and all their advice and Christian upbringing didn't stop me from being attacked. Right-living, as my father called it, seemed to lead me right into something wrong and my parents had yet to explain to me why it happened to me. If they hadn't pushed so hard to determine the path I would take for college, I wouldn't have pushed so hard against them in order to do something I wanted to do. My desire to sing was gone, so was my trust in God and especially the trust I had in my parents.

When we finally arrived, church was packed and we were barely able to get a good seat. Dad sits near the pulpit with the rest of the deacons, so getting a seat for him was no problem. I eventually got up and sat in the back. Didn't really want to be there anyway.

Pastor Jackson introduced the evangelist for the week then had the nerve to say he'd like to hear a solo from someone dear to his heart. Until he gets the okay, he won't call that person. I knew he was talking about me, but he won't get an okay from me this night. Not in this life, if I had anything to do with it.

The evangelist said his topic for the night was deliverance. Named a few things, even being delivered from self. That one perked my ears up and I listened attentively.

"Sometimes we live a life free of all general sins. We don't smoke, drink, cuss, lie, gossip, fornicate or be unfaithful in our marriages. In this we are confident that we are better than those who do these things and we will make it to Heaven based on the fact we lived a sin-free life. But what about being saved from you? You know you have that "I, mine and all mine" syndrome. Just because you don't do these obviously sinful things, you still must come to the realization that you need a Savior, and His name is Jesus Christ."

On and on he went about being delivered from yourself and habits you think are not sinful. He even touched on the fact that you cannot ride on someone else's salvation and make it in. Made me remember the talk I'd had with Pastor Jackson. I still couldn't get past the incident, and I guess I just didn't want to.

The evangelist made an altar call, and people went up for prayer. You can say the Spirit of God was moving in the place, but my heart wasn't touched. I decided right then that I wouldn't be coming back until Sunday, if then.

As soon as church was dismissed, I greeted a few folks, got the keys from my mother and ran to the car. I kept my hair over my face as I made my getaway. The second operation was successful in fully restructuring my jaw, but the thin line that started from just under my ear and almost to my chin was still very ugly to me. I refused to hold a conversation with anyone on my way out of the church because I didn't feel like smiling in anybody's face, trying to put on a facade. Please! I was so glad when we were able to go home. I told my parents I wouldn't be going to church until Sunday, but they asked every night anyway. It was the same routine; I would either be in the den or in my bedroom watching TV when my mother or father would ask me whether I planned to go to church. I wouldn't even look at them when I simply said, "no…" I gave them no explanation and they didn't ask for one, but there was a part of me that wished they did. Each day that week I fell deeper and deeper into depression, and by Friday morning of the same week my mother came to my room to talk to me.

"Tonya, are you giving up on God?" she asked, holding my hand.

"No, Mom. I'm just not ready to face this thing." I said, taking my hand from her.

"I'm worried about you." Her voice was filled with concern.

"I'll be okay, Mom. I just need some time to get through this," I said, lying down on my bed.

"Gary's going with us tonight. It's his first time," Mom said, trying to sound extra happy.

"He'll be all right without me there," I said, staring up at the ceiling.

"I hope you change your mind," my mother said, patting my knee.

"I don't think so," I answered, not looking at her.

It was eight in the morning. I had been up for two hours, eavesdropping on my parents as they discussed how they would try to get through to me. After my mother left, I slowly began my day. I got up and did the usual, take a bath, eat breakfast, lunch, watch TV and hide away in my room as much as I could. I didn't even get the mail out of the box anymore. The fall session for school would be starting in a few weeks, but I tore up any literature that came for me from Stamford/Brown College and had no plans to go anywhere else. The college offered to pay for my remaining semesters to make up for what Sam did to me, but my father had talked to his lawyer and he was handling all communications from the college. The lawyer was considering suing the college and Sam's family, but I wanted him to just leave it be because I had no intentions of going to court to testify.

While my parents were getting ready for church that evening, the doorbell rang. Since my mother had already told me that Gary would be going, I went ahead and answered the door. When I looked out of the window, it was Gary *and* his mother. I had to open the door since they saw me peek out. Mrs. Simmons hugged me tight, giving me a little kiss on my cheek. I hated this and rolled my eyes, looking up to the ceiling until she released me from her hug. I was grateful when my parents came downstairs. Gary introduced them to his mother while I eased away and back up to my room. Next thing I know, there's a knock on my door.

"Yes?"

"Tonya, it's Gary. Can I come in?"

I went to the door and parted it slightly. "What do you want?"

"I just wanted to see why you weren't going with us."

"Oh. I'm not feeling up to it."

That was all the explanation I was giving Gary. I know my mother told him to come up to my room to see if he could convince me to go to church, but it didn't work. I just told Gary that my father hated to be late for church, and pushed the door closed in his face and locked it. Then I grabbed the remote, got in bed and flicked channels until I found an old "I Love Lucy" episode. When the episode ended with Lucy's famous "Waaaaaah!" cry thirty minutes later and faded to a commercial, my TV started watching me.

The dream started again, but with more clarity than ever. First I heard Sam's wicked laugh echoing, and dark shadows started chasing me. I screamed, but when I ran, I would run right into Sam. He would say "obey the rules, obey the rules, Tonya!" Somehow I would get away, but then Sam would catch me again, dragging me by my hair. Holding me and sneering in my face, he raised his fist and it appeared to grow bigger as he lowered it to hit me. Several times his fist would come towards my face, and the sound of the fist landing upside my head sounded loudly in my ears. Each blow started coming faster and louder, and just before his fist crashed into my face I woke up screaming at the top of my lungs.

I lay on my bed listening to my heartbeat, afraid to move. Finally I reached over to the nightstand and turned on the light. I was crying and trembling as I pulled the comforter around me, but I kept hearing the sound of Sam's fist banging. Sitting up I realized that the banging sound was actually someone banging on the front door. The doorbell must have been ringing until the person decided to knock, but this was the first time I actually heard it. Then I heard a girl calling my name, begging me to open the door. I checked the clock on my nightstand and saw that my parents left for church an hour before, so I knew they weren't back. I slipped on a pair of jeans and headed for the front door. I turned the light on in the vestibule, and without looking through the window in the door, I asked who was there.

"It's me, Nicole! Please let me in, please! You've got to let me in…"

The panic in Nicole's voice was enough to make me unlock the door and let her in. No sooner than I'd gotten the door open, she ran into my arms, crying uncontrollably. Somehow I was able to maneuver around the hurting young girl to close the door and lock it. With my arm around Nicole's waist, I led her to the den, grabbing up tissues to help her wipe her tears.

Nicole's family joined our church about a year ago. Her mother, two brothers and little sister seemed to fit in well, but Nicole always looked like she would snap somebody's head off. She was in my Youth Department group, but she would never open up and talk with anyone. We would have different discussions on the issues of teen sex, drugs and such, and if Nicole said anything, she would complain about missing a party or not being with her boyfriend. After a while I just ignored her, realizing that she was just being a rebellious seventeen year-old, and hoping she would get it together eventually.

When Nicole's crying became sniffles, I tried to soothe her by softly rubbing her back and asking her to tell me what was wrong. Her mother attended services faithfully, so I also wondered why she wasn't at church with her family. Nicole sat up, wiped the new tears that were sliding down her cheeks, stared straight ahead and told me what happened to her.

"My mother told me we had to go to church, but my friend was having a house party. I promised I would be there because my boyfriend and his friends were going to be there too. So, I told my mother that I was going over my friend's house so she could help me with math homework and that I would come to church after that. But I lied. I took my change of clothes in my book bag and changed for the party when I got there. Only I didn't think they were going to be doing drugs there. I knew they were going to be drinking beer, but smoking weed and somebody had cocaine and ecstasy...anyway, my boyfriend got high and tried to take me in a back room to have sex, but I didn't want to, so he started pushing me and hitting on me. When he started calling me out of my name, I just gathered my things and left. The next thing I know, he was in his car and started chasing me!"

Nicole stopped to let some more tears fall, burying her face in her hands. Still I didn't say anything; I just put my arm around her and wiped her tears. She composed herself and said she thought her boyfriend was going to kill her. Somehow she found herself running down my street, and remembered where I lived. She thought everyone would be at church but she saw the reflection of the TV through my window. That's when she ran up on the porch banging on the door, pleading for me to let her in.

"How did you know I was home? Not that I make a habit of leaving the TV on when I'm not here," I asked Nicole.

"I saw your car in the driveway and I figured the same thing about the TV. What I don't understand is how things turned out so crazy tonight. I know I disobeyed my mother and lied to her, but I didn't deserve this. My boyfriend has never treated me like this."

At first I didn't know how to answer her question because it had been one of my own for that last few months. But I also realized Nicole was hurting and there had to be something I could do for her or say to make her feel better. I put my concerns on the back burner and focused on Nicole. I put myself in her place.

"Do you realize that there are things in life that are going to happen no matter what? And then there are things that will happen because of the choices we make in life...sometimes we are forewarned about the consequences, and sometimes we aren't aware of what they can be until something happens. Yet trials and tribulations are a part of life; they are what help to make us who we are. It's how we respond to them that will determine how we will come out of it. You can blame your boyfriend, your friend or your mother for what happened to you tonight, but I am convinced that nothing happens without God knowing it. Who more than He wants the best for us? It's just that sometimes we have to go through something in order to come to the realization that no matter what we go through, it's all in the making of us. The thing is, we have to make up our minds to either serve God or not. There is no in between, because if we try to live in the middle of things, it won't be long before we know it will not work." I was explaining this to Nicole, as well as myself. "I must also say that there are gifts and talents that God has placed in us for a specific time, and we must use them for Him. Sometimes we get a little off track, but it's these very same trials we have that actually help us get back on the right road."

All this time my family, friends and church family had been trying so hard to get me out of my funk and the answer was always within me. It felt great to speak the very words that would allow me to see my situation for what it truly is! Then suddenly I felt like a weight had lifted from my shoulders and I told Nicole that we should head on over to the church for the last night of the revival. It was close to nine-fifteen and I wanted to get there before they dismissed. We both went to my room as I hurried to dress, digging around for my car keys because I haven't driven since the attack. We were pretty late, but I knew that I had to be there. I actually wanted to be there.

When we arrived, there were a few people at the altar with the evangelist who was still ministering to them. I asked the usher if she knew where my mother was sitting, and she led me to her. A few folks had to slide over. I gave Nicole a tight hug and made my way to a seat next to my mother, and she went in another direction to find a seat next to her mother.

"Tonya, I'm so glad you came!" my mother said, hugging me to her. It really felt good to receive her hug, so I hugged her back.

Then the evangelist continued to speak because he said the Lord wasn't through blessing. While he was still talking and ministering to the people who were at the altar, I felt like I couldn't keep my seat because of a new feeling of freedom I felt. The urge to go to the altar was so strong in my heart. I got up and made my way there. The evangelist didn't have to tell me to raise my hands. I couldn't help but to surrender to the power of God. His anointing fell on me in a way I had never experienced before. All I could do was praise God and thank Him for all He had done for me.

As the evangelist placed his hand on my head, he prayed for me, and told me that I have to give all of me for all of God. When he asked me had I made up my mind to do just that, with tears streaming down my face I said, "Yes, yes I have, yes I have!"

Before returning to my seat, I felt so compelled to share my testimony of how I'd been blessed to make it out with my life after the attack at school. I shared the downside of it, but I also told how through helping someone else, I came to realize that what means the most to me is my commitment to God, family and friends.

As I was about to take my seat, the evangelist told me three more times to go and be blessed. I knew that I was blessed without a doubt. I could put the incident behind me and live my life the way I'm supposed to live, for God and unto Him.

Pastor Jackson got up to dismiss the service and asked me to come and close out with a song. I did something I had never done before, first pray and ask God what to sing. Then, I closed my eyes and sang it directly to Him.

The song started out with "One man sat alone beside the highway begging," but my favorite part: "He'll take your gloom and fill your life with glory!!!"

God has done so much for me and I will always praise His name. I have vowed that for the rest of my life I will serve Him with my whole heart.

# Everything I Need

*"According as his divine power hath given unto us all things that pertain unto life and godliness, through the knowledge of him that hath called us to glory and virtue."*

*2 Peter 1:3 KJV*

# Chapter Eight

The clock on the dashboard seemed to flash a new minute by the second. I was late in picking Lisa up from the airport, and I knew she would be pacing back and forth. I smiled to myself as I saw Lisa in my mind's eye, cigarette in hand, short skirt, high heel shoes, flipping her shoulder length hair over her shoulder when she stopped to see if she could spot me coming towards her. Ever since Lisa moved to California, she had become so impatient! It was either now or never, but because she was coming for my wedding *and* is my Maid of Honor, she will wait until I get there. It won't hurt her to wait an extra fifteen minutes. She would wait as much as an hour for me when I had chores to do when we were growing up.

In a way, Lisa's impatience started back when we were kids in junior high school. She couldn't wait to kiss a boy, have a real boyfriend and have sex. She was the first of my friends to become sexually active, automatically making her think she was experienced enough to tell us how and what to do. It didn't take long for the novelty of talking about it to wear off, but when she did share with us, she sounded more like an adult than a teenager. I never told her, but I viewed her differently, more mature than I could ever be at fourteen years old. I might have felt this way because she told me more than she told Denise or Sasha, and that was because she was closer to me than either of them. Although there was a time I wondered if she was truly a friend to me because she didn't have time to deal with me and my issues. Could be that she didn't know how. After Sam attacked me, it wasn't long before Lisa stopped coming over to see about me, or call me on the phone.

When Lisa first found out what happened to me, she was ready to leave school and come home to beat Sam down. Although she was a junior in college, confrontation and getting people straight was still pretty much a part of who Lisa was, so I wasn't surprised to hear that was her reaction. But by the time I had the second surgery on my jaw to reconstruct it, Lisa had all but stopped visiting me a few weeks into my recovery. I'd developed a nasty attitude that would keep anyone away, but I never thought my best friend would forget all about me. Especially during a time that I felt I needed her most, causing me to resent the times that I never turned my back on Lisa, even to the point of lying for her on more than one occasion.

Suddenly a car horn blew, bringing my attention back to driving, a green light in front of me and the road leading into the airport. I blew my horn back and took off, reading signs as I went along to find the right terminal and airline I was to meet Lisa. Sure enough as I pulled up in front of the airline, Lisa was pacing back and forth, smoking her cigarette and checking her watch. I pulled up laughing because my thoughts of my friend was more than a little accurate, only I had no idea that she would be wearing the outfit she had on. She wore a short, black sheer dress that had small slits over most of it. Underneath she had on a solid black body suit that appeared to have an extra dip in it to reveal her cleavage. She accessorized her outfit with a pair of silver sling back shoes and clutch purse, diamond earrings and a diamond pendant necklace. I didn't understand why she would want to look like that and be in the company of nothing but women.

Before I could get out of the car, Lisa was pulling one of her suitcases towards the back of my car, and I was still laughing out loud.

"What is so funny? I'm standing out here for fifteen minutes longer than I intended to be, and you find something funny?" Lisa wanted to know as we embraced.

"It didn't hurt you to wait a few minutes. Besides, we don't want to be the first ones to arrive at the shower, do we?" I asked, grabbing one of Lisa's suitcases and placing it in the trunk.

"Whatever...but why does it have to be at the church?"

"You would ask that after you put on that outfit," I said, as a few men walked by, looking at Lisa up and down, smiling. One of them winked his eye and licked his lips!

"This is nothing compared to the other outfits I have. Besides, do you really think I'm going to come back home and not look better than every woman I know?" Lisa got into the car while flashing those guys a smile.

Lisa started filling me in on her complaints about her fiancé as we drove towards the church. I looked forward to the times I could share with my best friend face-to-face instead of on the phone. We kept in touch as much as our busy schedules would allow. We had set up certain times to call each other so we wouldn't waste money calling only to find the other not at home because of the time difference between the east and west coasts. I'd long ago gotten a separate line in my room, and Lisa and I would spend at least an hour on the phone, laughing and carrying on like we did back in high school. When we both got e-mail, we would keep in touch that way, and when instant messaging became the thing, it was like we were writing notes in high school.

As long as Lisa had been engaged, I thought for sure she would have been married long before me, but she said just living with her fiancé was enough for now. She couldn't spend too much time with him because he was still in med school. Their schedules conflict terribly and she said she's still not sure she could handle being the wife of a doctor no matter how good the money would be. The truth is, Lisa and her fiancé hit a lot of bumps in their relationship during college. Lisa wanted someone steady in her life and she wanted to play around too. She went through a lot of changes during those years, experimenting with marijuana, hanging out in clubs and ending up in some guy's bed, admitting that she didn't remember how she got there. Her boyfriend didn't know about most of Lisa's crazy ways at first, and when he did find out, they parted ways for a while, then reconciling, only to have heated arguments. Lisa made up her mind to be faithful and stop playing games, but their relationship became rocky again when Lisa went through the weight loss thing, becoming addicted to diet pills by her senior year in college. To lose weight, she stopped eating while taking the pills and got very sick. Sasha came to their dorm room after classes and found Lisa balled up in pain on her bed. Lisa was shaken up pretty good when the doctor in the emergency room told her she had to stop taking those pills, explaining how dangerous they really were. Needing something to fill the void of the pills and the marijuana, Lisa turned to smoking cigarettes. She does not take the pills any more, but she will fast three or four days at a time to keep her weight down, to stay in a slender size eight. Lisa claims she does this so the clothes she designs will look better. I feel it's because she had never been that small in her life.

Lisa usually visited from California for two weeks in July each summer, but she gave up one of her weeks in July to be home for my wedding. Every time Lisa came home, she would change her look. Her hair and, or dress to suit the mood she happened to be in at the time. Last summer Lisa sported a very short afro dyed red! When she came home the first week of July this year, she had shoulder length hair and wore it in a flip hairstyle with a few streaks of blond here and there. I'd hoped that if there was a change between July and now, it wouldn't be something weird, or "radical" as Lisa called it. Thankfully there was no change.

Lisa was having the same career conflict she had since high school, draw and write comics or pursue fashion design. Although she had gone to college for fashion design, Lisa found it difficult to break into the market without working for someone else. Determined to make a name for herself, Lisa worked for a comic book company while creating and making dress styles. She had no problem wearing them, even if they didn't cover up too much of her body.

We arrived at the church and used the entrance from the outside of the church that led to the basement and the dining hall. As we walked along the hallway there were balloons and streamers in the colors of my wedding, or at least as close as they could get. I guess it is kind of hard trying to find teal blue balloons, so blue and off-white balloons did the trick. As we entered the doorway of the fellowship hall, a big sign with blue letters, "Congratulations Tonya! We Love You!" with streamers and balloons around it. One of the mothers in my church greeted me and announced that I'd arrived, handing us off to another woman in my church who led us to a long table at the front of the hall.

My seat was in the center of the table, and all of the chairs faced the room so that I could see all of my guests. My chair had helium balloons on them with expressions of love and well wishes on them, as well as streamers and a special place setting in front of me. My mother, both grandmothers, Lisa, Sasha and Denise shared the table with me. A small, round table was set up close by that continued to grow with presents of all shapes and colors. The larger gifts had to be placed on the floor near the table. I was amazed at the number of people who had turned out.

When my mother stood up and tapped her fork on the side of her glass, the bridal shower officially began. After she spoke for a few minutes, my mother turned the bridal shower responsibilities over to Lisa just as Sasha and Denise made their way to our table. With their help, Lisa and a few more young ladies created a circle with some chairs, and then put me in the middle in a chair by myself so we could play some games. We played some traditional bridal shower games like "Guess", a cute clear bottle filled with sweet tarts, my guests having to guess how many were in there for a prize. Then we played "Who Knows the Bride Best" and "Who Knows the Groom Best." Lisa, Sasha and Denise decided not to participate in these games to give everyone else a chance, since they knew *everything* about me. They joined when the "Toilet Paper Game" began. Then, everyone expressed her love for me.

At one point I was sure I would get a pat on the head from one of my grandmothers.

We walked back down memory lane to when I was a baby up until my adult years, but not without my mother saying how proud she was that I returned to school. Her eyes got a little misty because there was a time neither of us believed I would continue to live, much less return to school.

When we finished the last game, Lisa told everyone to take a seat. Dinner was served buffet style, mainly finger foods, and, my favorite, yellow cake with butter cream frosting and fresh strawberries and cream that melted in my mouth. After my first piece, I wrapped a piece to take home for later that night, but I started picking at it before it was time to open my gifts.

Some of the gifts I received were the traditional ones for the home, but what amazed me the most were the many sets of sexy lingerie! My friends would buy something like that, but the women in my church?

Unbelievable! Every color imaginable, in different shapes, sizes and colors, including crotch less panties! Someone even gave me a pack of batteries! I just laughed along with everyone else.

I stayed behind and watched my friends and a few others clean up. According to Lisa, the bride-to-be should concentrate on being the bride, so I sat back and made mental notes to add to the list of things I needed Lisa to take care of as my Maid of Honor.

As soon as we finished at the church, we piled the gifts into my car and took them to my house. Lisa rushed to take the gifts inside because she was meeting Sasha so they could go out to a club. I should have known her outfit was meant to do more than make a few women jealous at a bridal shower. My father helped us to stack the gifts in the den and after walking Lisa to the door, I headed upstairs, pulling off my shoes and loosening the buttons on my dress. Though I was completely exhausted after undressing, bathing and preparing for bed, I couldn't fall asleep. There was nothing worth watching on TV, so I turned it back off only to find myself tossing and turning a few times. Still unable to go to sleep, I got up and turned on my computer and entered the details from my bridal shower into my diary. A quick smile and even a few stomach laughs escaped me as I thought back on the shower and especially the gifts, noting who gave me what gifts. After I finished entering the additions to my journal, I climbed into bed with a big smile on my face.

• • •

Counting on Lisa to be here for me was the best thing I could have done. She helped keep me grounded, stopping the unnecessary worries or hysteria. We actually started having fun, which reminded me of our childhood. The Wednesday leading up to my wedding, we were in my room putting flowers on the tiny bottles of bubbles that would be the favors handed to the guests as they arrived for the wedding. We were laughing and carrying on like we did in high school, giggling and rolling on the floor, tears streaming down our faces.

"On a serious note, Tonya, how has Sasha been doing? I don't get to talk to her too much since she left Cali, and I didn't want her to feel uncomfortable the other night at dinner by asking her anything too personal," said Lisa, holding a bottle of bubbles up to the light.

"She still looks good, and as far as I know, she's doing fine. I have taken the same approach as you have, and don't ask her too many questions. One thing for sure, Sasha has come a long way with living with her condition and not letting it rule her life. I'm sure if there is a change, she will tell us, right?"

"Yeah, I guess…but I want her to know that I'm always here for her. I still don't know what to say to her, especially now that so much time has gone by since college."

My friends and I have hung in there with Sasha over the years, especially when things hit the fan concerning Sasha's condition. Right after finals in our junior year in high school, Sasha attempted suicide by taking pills from a bottle of her mother's painkillers. I remember how I just stood helpless, unable to move while the paramedics tended to her. Sometimes I can still hear her mother calling Sasha's name in that high pitch scream of hers. When Lisa, Denise and I went to see her a few days later in the hospital, it was then that she told us of her HIV status. She told us that James Barnett had told her that he loved her; that he had never told that to any other girl. James convinced her to have sex with him by telling her the same thing he told me when we dated, that he always used protection with the other girls he slept with. But in the heat of passion, he didn't use a condom.

When she heard the rumors around school about the spread of AIDS, she took the test as a precaution not considering that for one minute she had anything. It wasn't until she was called to the nurse's office to be informed of James' status that she dreaded receiving the results of her own test. When it came back positive, she withdrew from all of us because she was embarrassed, and convinced she was going to die anyway, the only thing she could think of was to take her own life.

We spent time with Sasha that day, encouraging her, crying with her and promising to always be there for her to help her through this. I even told her I believed that since her condition had not progressed from the virus to AIDS, there is a good chance she would be cured. I don't think I did a good job convincing her because I had a hard time trying to believe my own words. The first few months after Sasha came out the hospital were difficult, but as promised, Lisa, Denise and I stayed close to Sasha, giving her some extra love and finding ways to try to put her illness as far away as we could in light of the circumstances.

The one thing I couldn't bring myself to do was to tell my parents about Sasha, especially since that night at church when it seemed the whole city turned out to hear what my Pastor had to say about HIV and AIDS, and the way my mother flipped out after hearing that message on the answering machine about James. I just didn't know how she would react to the news that one of her daughter's friends had the HIV virus. Since I didn't know, I wasn't taking any chances on telling her any time soon. At least not right away because Sasha was still having a hard time dealing with it.

A week before we were to go back to school for our senior year of high school, the four of us were in the den at my house going through the clothes we bought at the mall, laughing and having a good time when Lisa's mother came over to talk to my mother. As the two women passed by the den to go sit in the kitchen, Mrs. James stopped by the door and asked Sasha how she had been feeling. Sasha was immediately embarrassed, but out of respect she told Mrs. James she was feeling fine. My mother made eye contact with me and I just hunched my shoulders because I was not going to say anything else to make Sasha feel bad. Just before my mother and Mrs. James reached the kitchen, we heard Lisa's mother say, "Tonya hasn't mentioned anything to you about Sasha? I sure thought you knew…"

The fun we were having was interrupted and we all sat in silence. What could we possibly say? Then Sasha started gathering her belongings and, without a word, left the den and my house. Lisa started apologizing for her mother and followed behind Sasha, who was in tears. Denise quickly came up with an excuse of her own to leave. I grabbed up my bags and went to my room to put away the clothes I bought, and waited at my desk for my mother to confront me as soon as Mrs. James left. I pulled out a note pad so I could keep busy and distracted until my mother came upstairs. All I did was scribble, draw stick figures and write my name all over the page.

Sure enough, as soon as I heard my mother telling Lisa's mother she will see her later, I heard her footsteps. Knocking on my door as she opened it, my mother came in and looked at me, waiting for me to say something. I didn't even know how to begin.

"How long were you going to wait to tell me about Sasha? Lillian tells me the girl is HIV positive. Is that right?" asked my mother as she put her hands on her hips.

"Yes, Mom…" I said, twisting the bottom of my shirt, and walked to the bed.

"Did you also know that she got the disease from having sex with that boy James your father never approved of? You must have known that since she is your friend. Oh, and when she attempted suicide a few months ago, it had nothing to do with her mother but that she didn't want to live anymore..."

"Mom! Sasha made a bad decision and I don't take it lightly, I don't...it's just that we promised that we would be there for her and I can't turn my back on her. Plus Sasha told me not to tell anyone. She made a mistake, Mom, one that anyone could have made. I just didn't know how to tell you, that's all," I said, my eyes filling with tears.

"Tonya, you could have told me about it. I don't like to hear something like this from someone else. Do you think it would change the way I feel about Sasha? Do you?" My mother sat next to me on the bed. "Because it doesn't...I know she's a good friend of yours, and the last thing I would do is make her feel uncomfortable about her situation. What I'm trying to get across to you is that I should have known about it before Lillian came over here telling me as if she knows everything about the HIV virus and Sasha."

"Okay, Mom, I understand what you're saying. I wish I had told you because Lisa's mother didn't even wait until she got in the kitchen before we heard her say she would tell you about Sasha. It wasn't fair to Sasha at all!" I said, the tears streaming down my face now as I buried my head in my mother's chest.

My mother hugged me and comforted me, but also told me I had to tell my father about Sasha when he came home from work that evening. I had a few hours to think about how I would tell him, which only made it harder to come up with the words when he did come in. I waited until he got comfortable in his favorite chair with his newspaper before I went into the den. Nothing I practiced came out when I opened my mouth, I just blurted out that Sasha was HIV positive and that she contracted it from the guy James I used to date. My father slowly folded his newspaper, got up out of his chair and paced the floor a few times, then came and stood in front of me. He looked at me and started to say something, thought better of it and paced the floor some more. My father walked back to his chair and sitting down explained that the last thing he ever wanted to do was to pick my friends, but what happened to Sasha was proof that he should meet everyone I called a friend.

"Not that I don't want you to have Sasha for a friend, but what does that say about her if she goes out and have sex unprotected with all that's out there today?"

"Dad, it was just once. Sasha didn't know that James had anything...he took advantage of her."

"He took advantage of her? She couldn't tell him 'no'? She still had a choice, Tonya!"

"Dad, I know she did, but..."

"But what? Do you really think there is an excuse for this? Ok, maybe I'm being hard, but Tonya, this shouldn't have ever happened! This girl is what, sixteen? What's going to happen to her if they never find a cure? What if they find one but the disease is in a stage where the cure can't help her? She's going to die! And for what? And for what, Tonya?" He got up from his chair to pace the floor some more. I sat there looking at my hands because I didn't have any answers, and most certainly, I couldn't answer for Sasha.

As far as boys were concerned, he wanted me to understand that he had to know all about them, even if they were just friends. My father told me that there was more to a friendship with a guy than sex and that this situation with Sasha should serve to prove to me that some choices in life could cost me my life. Even though my father said I could still be friends with Sasha, I still felt like someone forced all the air out of my lungs.

*134*

Finally he said, "I knew that boy was trouble. I'm not glad about what has happened to Sasha, but I tell you this...and I must be truthful...I'm glad it isn't you." My father turned his back to me and went into the kitchen to talk to my mother while she finished preparing dinner.

Somehow I was able to convince Sasha that my parents did not judge her or would treat her any different. At least going back to school that fall to start our senior year in high school helped Sasha a lot. At first, she considered transferring to a school out of the district where no one knew her or heard about her situation. We convinced her that most people thought it was a rumor. We all had Sasha's back whenever someone was bold enough to ask either of us. Denise decided not to entertain any questions by ignoring them or changing the subject. Lisa ended up telling people off, and I would tell them to ask Sasha, and she told them to check themselves to see if the rumor was about them.

The hardest part for Sasha was being afraid to go to sleep at night. She always feared that she would die in her sleep, so she sat up on her pillows as opposed to lying down in her bed. She would cry herself to sleep and cry when she awoke in the morning, grateful for another day of life. This went on all through our senior year in high school; the reason I know it did is because Sasha's eyes were always very puffy in the mornings. Sometimes she would look so sad, I was near tears, but once we all had a chance to talk and start laughing, Sasha's spirits would pick up, and we would make it through another day.

We were bored at lunch one day during the second week of school and decided to go outside for some air at Sasha's insistence. As self-conscious as she'd become, I was surprised she made the suggestion. As soon as we walked out of the cafeteria doors, Sasha looked around to see who was there, and then led the way to a tree a short distance away.

While we stood there, a guy neither of us had ever met walked over and introduced himself. It wasn't hard to notice someone new at our school because there were only about 800 students. We knew most of our graduating class because we had all gone through school together since kindergarten, and the other students all lived nearby.

"What's up? My name is Quadir Jones," he said, taking off his cap showing his shiny, black wavy hair. His teeth were clean, and one of the front ones was chipped. He smelled so good! Slim and somewhat lanky, he was cute and very friendly. We introduced ourselves and fell into easy conversation with Quadir. He had moved here over the summer from New York and didn't really know anyone. He hung outside during lunch to meet people. While Quadir talked, he kept his eyes on Sasha. She had gained the weight back she lost after her suicide attempt, and had her hair cut very low and curled tight for school. Sasha is pretty, so I wasn't surprised she captured Quadir's attention right from the start.

The bell rang and we started heading for our next class when Quadir called Sasha back. I walked slowly so I could be nosy and hear what Quadir wanted. He actually asked Sasha if she would like to catch a movie some time. I wondered if Sasha would go and if so, would she tell him about her illness? In the weeks that followed, the friendship between Sasha and Quadir continued to grow. It wasn't strange to see the two of them walking arm in arm down the hall to their classes, or standing outside of the cafeteria sharing some private time. I was really happy that Sasha met Quadir because he helped her to get through the rough times.

We found out later during the school year that Quadir was extra understanding to Sasha's condition because his mother contracted HIV some years earlier from a blood transfusion before blood was being checked for the disease. Sasha said it didn't have anything to do with how they felt about each other. To prove his eternal friendship, Quadir gave Sasha a friendship ring. She came in the cafeteria that day, smiling from ear-to-ear. Denise saw her and commented, "Here comes 'Mrs. Quadir now."

"That's right, I'm here! And do I have something to show y'all," said Sasha.

"She's cheesin' all hard, so something is definitely up," Lisa said, turning sideways in her chair to show she wasn't interested.

"Yeah Lisa, take a good look at this rock on my hand. I know y'all jeal," said Sasha, holding out her left hand to show us a small friendship ring. The diamond wasn't big, but the ring was really nice and Sasha seemed happier than she had been in a long time.

"Girl, what did you do to get that?" asked Denise, snatching Sasha's hand. She held the ring up to the light to see the stone, and then smiled at Sasha. "I think it's sweet Quadir shows you that he values your friendship."

Sasha took a seat at the table with us, holding her hand out at different angles admiring her ring while the rest of us ate and watched her. She was wearing a knee-length gold colored skirt with a black blouse, buttoned down the back, and a pair of short black patent leather pumps. Her hair seemed to shine a little brighter as she paused to pat her neat curls before going back to the task of admiring her ring.

"So why did he buy the ring? It has to be something to all this," Lisa said before she took another bite of her sandwich.

Sasha explained that she and Quadir had made a trip to the mall the evening before, and stopped at one of the jewelry stores. He had already picked it out, but took Sasha along for her approval. It was more than obvious she approved the way she was looking at her ring under the light, and we were all happy for her. As much as Lisa tried to play it off, she was happy for Sasha as well. She just liked to bust on Sasha a lot.

Sasha stopped admiring her ring long enough to tell Lisa that Quadir had a friend who wanted to meet her.

"Oh, for real? Who is he?" Lisa asked, eyes lighting up with interest.

"Look at you, acting like you ain't never had a man. Anyway, his name is Terrence and he wants us to get together for a movie this weekend...if you wanna go," while holding her ring up to the light again.

"You know I do," said Lisa.

"Okay, I'll set it up. Now we have to work on 'Miss Goody Two Shoes' over here," Sasha said, smiling at me.

"Whatever...when the time comes, I'll meet the guy for me. Trust me, I ain't in no kind of hurry," I said, dismissing Sasha's comment.

The bell rang and Lisa and Sasha headed off together so that Sasha could fill her in on Terrence and their plans for the movie. I walked along to class alone with a smile on my face, feeling better about Sasha than I had in a long while. I hoped Sasha was truly happy and that things with Quadir would last longer than a school year like most teen-age relationships. Worrying if her HIV status would turn to full-blown AIDS had to be hard on Sasha because it was hard on me trying to smile and act normal every day and I wasn't the one suffering from the disease. But she was beginning to handle it well, and I really believed that Quadir helped her a lot in that short time. Senior year was almost over, and all we had left were the prom, finals and graduation. Until then, I used to view Lisa as the adult among us, but it was Sasha who was becoming the adult by learning to cope with a bigger than adult-sized problem.

• • •

In preparing for the prom, the four of us had to agree on a color scheme. Sasha wanted to make a statement with neon yellow, Denise wanted to wear the most revealing dress she could find, and Lisa wanted to wear black. I told them all we should choose colors that would compliment each other so that when we walked into the ballroom that would be the first thing everyone would notice.

The night of the prom my house was filled to the brim with stockings, shoes, perfume, hairspray, last minute nail polish touch-ups and my mother running up and downstairs trying to keep from burning my father's dinner while she helped my friends and me to get ready. I don't know why I agreed that we could all get dressed at my house. Thank God for the extra bathroom downstairs, or we would have been much later than thirty minutes.

Lisa wore a pretty off the shoulder eggshell colored gown that had two pieces of fabric sashaying across each other in the front. The front of the dress fell just below her knees, while the back dipped just a little further down. She wore pumps the exact color as her dress, having to have them dyed, and a thin knitted shawl to cover her arms.

Sasha wore a form fitting, pastel green dress. It was a strapless number with a sheer matching long sleeve dress over top of it. Shoes died to match, as well as a clutch purse, pearl earrings and necklace, and a freshly cut, permed hairdo. She practiced in front of the mirror how she planned to dance with Quadir while we all screamed at her to move so we could use the mirror too.

Ever since Denise and Johnny started dating, her style of dress changed dramatically. No more weird colors, oversized, frumpy outfits. Everything became form fitting and showed a lot of skin. Denise's dress was a silky teal blue with the back out. She wore a pair of high-heeled patent leather black pumps, and carried a matching clutch and found some earrings that matched perfectly with her dress.

There was no way I could wear a halter or show too much of my cleavage without my father having a stroke. He felt there was no reason a young woman should have most of her body parts showing, so I finally settled on a below the knees light peach dress with spaghetti strings and a matching sheer dress to cover it. My mother approved of it while we were in the store, but my father had a fit until my mother described the other dresses I wanted to buy. I found a pair of peach shoes, and found accessories with peach and pearls for my ears and my neck.

We were still making last minute adjustments and fussing over our hair. We carried on so much up in my room that we practically forgot that we actually had dates coming to pick us up. When we were all finished getting dressed and after my mother called to us three times, we came down the stairs like divas just bursting on the scene. The guys were handsome in their tuxedos, cummerbunds and bow ties to match their date's dress. My father was going crazy with his camera while the long white stretch limo waited for us outside. Our neighbors were standing outside oooohing and aaaaahing at us, while camera flashes continued all around us. I felt like we were celebrities who just blew up. Our chauffeur helped us get in the limo then we drove to the plushest hotel I'd ever been in.

The Excelsior Promenade was just forty-five miles away, in a town called Binghamton. The place was simply gorgeous. The lobby had a huge crystal chandelier, surrounded by about four smaller ones. The color scheme was peach, green and white, with expensive looking artwork lining the walls just right. Everything looked so lavish, and the staff was very nice. We were actually escorted to the ballroom. It wasn't the hotel's biggest ballroom, but it was beautiful. The tables were set up on either side of the room so that the middle of the floor could be used for dancing, and a dais set up for the officers of our graduation class, our principal and a host of other important people. The DJ was playing Luther Vandross' "Bad Boy/Having a Party." We found our table and got comfortable. Quadir took Sasha out to the dance floor while the rest of us discussed how beautiful everything was and waved at or spoke to people who came to our table.

"Can you believe this, Lisa? Now this is the way to end senior year," I said, looking around the room. I was almost in awe at how classy and elegant everything was.

"And you know it! I'm going to dance until these heels hurt my feet, and I'm going to eat until I can't eat no more," said Lisa. Then she leaned over close to me to whisper in my ear, "So where are you and Gary going after we leave here?"

"What do you mean?" I asked, pretending I didn't know what she was talking about.

"Don't play with me, Tonya, you know."

The DJ changed the music sparing me the embarrassment of telling my friend that I would not be participating in the "after-prom" activities that usually go on. We all headed for the dance floor as the lyrics to Tupac's "California Love" started pumping through the speakers. In between dances we took time for the appetizer, main course and dessert, but most of the night we were on the floor dancing to tunes ranging from Mary J. Blige's "Be Happy" to Biggie's more popular songs.

Before night's end, we made it over to the corner where the photographer was set up. He had a vase with big flowers on a tall stand, and the wall to set the background for the picture. The photographer had us take a few poses together and then individually, showing us how to pose for each shot. The DJ told us that we would remember this night always and forever as he slipped into Luther Vandross' remake of Heat Wave's classic "Always and Forever" for the last dance of the evening. I knew I would never forget this night because, to me, it marked the beginning of adulthood and my independence.

After the prom, the limo dropped each couple at the guy's home. I was a bit nervous and yet excited because I knew I wanted to spend time with Gary without him hoping for some "after-prom" activities. We all went our separate ways. Lisa and Terrence were taking a ride down to Atlantic City for the weekend. Sasha and Quadir headed into New York to cruise around and find a hotel to stay in for the night just to talk and then go sightseeing the next day. Denise and Johnny went to the local Holiday Inn.

I sensed that Gary knew by the way they danced with their dates that Lisa and Denise were sexually active. Their dancing was suggestively sexual, holding each other as close as they could. Most of the other students danced this way with their faces held close together; and hands remained on waistlines only because of the presence of chaperones walking by to monitor where the guys put their hands. The closest Gary got to me was when I turned around because I was feeling the beat of Mary J. Blige's "You Bring Me Joy." As Gary caressed my waist and gently pulled me toward him, I stiffened. Not like panic, but nervous and I guess it sent some sort of warning because he rubbed against me for a one-two-one-two of the beat and then coolly backed away.

As Gary drove away from his house, I told him that I didn't have to be in until two a.m. so we could go somewhere. But he did not seem impressed or eager. I have never managed to get a good read of Gary's facial expressions. He was able to think the worst while maintaining a cool, unflustered look unless he was angry past the point of no return. At that moment, quietly riding through the dark town on prom night, I felt like a little girl because I was not, as some other girls had decided, going to become a woman. Or what these girls believed what becoming a woman was. As we drove in Gary's car, even though I could not see his eyes and their aim, I could sense that Gary regretted my being his prom date. I started feeling this way while the DJ played slower and more suggestive songs and couples hugged closer, and there was this space, this distance between Gary and me.

In my mind it was the epitome of romance–a young man and a young woman, hand in hand, dancing, in unison in a semi-dark, huge ballroom; dressed to a tee, daydreaming and holding onto the last bastion of youth, slowly walking toward the edge, toward becoming a man and becoming a woman. But there was a distance between Gary and me that my words couldn't break through. As we passed the cars filled with other students calling out their windows to other students they passed along the way, I felt the distance growing. Our car was missing their jovial mood. The prom was a great start to the night and I was looking forward to a nice end to the night. There was no special place to go in our town because it was mostly residential. If you wanted to go somewhere to have fun, you would go into New York or a few towns over depending on what you were looking to do. The more we drove around and talked, our conversation became blander because Gary never looked my way, as if trying to maintain or increase the distance between us.

"Mind if I park up at The Hill?" Gary finally looked in my direction. "I don't want to ride around until time for you to be home."

"No...no I don't mind."

When Gary found a parking space, he turned the car off but left the radio on, the music seemingly filling in where our words failed.

"Oooh, this is my song," I said as Whitney Houston belted out "I'll Always Love You." I sang along while Gary just listened. There was still no conversation, just the next song and Gary leaning back in his seat. I tried to bring back the good feeling I had at the prom. "So have you decided which scholarship you're going to accept?"

"Yeah...I have an internship with BAN, a telecommunications company. It's part of the scholarship I accepted and the best one," Gary answered, wiping over his head, a nervous habit.

"Really? That is so good! I don't know what I'm going to be doing this summer," I said, the reality of my statement hitting me hard.

"Have you been accepted to any colleges?"

"Yes, I've been accepted to a few, but my parents are still trippin' about me singing."

"You don't have to declare your major right away."

"I know, but my parents are on me to find something other than singing in case I don't make it."

"With your voice, there's no way you won't," Gary said, almost whispering.

We talked until it was time to head home, something I was grateful for because I didn't want such a beautiful night to end on a bad note. I still did not know why he got quiet on me at first, and I was feeling a little disappointed because Gary didn't ask for a kiss all night, but it was really good to just sit and talk. He did hold my hand from time to time as if he was being careful not to overstep his bounds.

When we got to my house, we stood on the porch for a while, neither of us saying a word at first. My parents left the porch light on for me, and I was a little nervous about kissing Gary goodnight.

"Tonya, I really enjoyed being with you tonight," Gary said after clearing his throat.

"I enjoyed being with you, too. I had no idea you were such a gentleman."

"And a scholar," said Gary and we laughed.

144

We stood on the porch, not saying anything, feeling that this moment may be goodbye forever. Finally I broke the silence. "Do you think we'll get together again some time?"

"Yeah...I'll call you."

"Well, I'd better go in. Good night, Gary." Then I did something I never thought I would have the nerve to do. I kissed Gary on his cheek. He took my hand, pulled me to him, kissing me by sharing his tongue with me. Then he outlined my lips lightly with his tongue and then slowly, sensually began to take my tongue again. When we were through, I was literally breathless!

"Well, I-I'd better go in," I stammered, as if drunk from my first real kiss.

Gary kissed me one more time and I finally went in. My parents were in the den and asked me to come and share my evening with them. I told them everything except that Gary and I kissed. Couldn't tell them that! But we sat up, until about four in the morning, talking and laughing.

Throughout the summer after we graduated from high school, Gary and I dated often and spent lots of idle time together. We had gotten into a zone where I wasn't being pressured for sex, and he wasn't asking.

That is, he didn't ask until a few days before he was due to leave for college in California. I almost gave up my virginity that night, but thankfully I didn't. He went off to college and I stayed home and went to college locally. We agreed to just be friends. The love I had for Gary continued to grow, even when we couldn't decide what kind of relationship we wanted to have with each other. That summer, I also came to realize Gary liked to play mind games, and I was determined to stay ahead of his games.

I considered my relationship with Gary to be more than just a high school crush, and he took advantage of my naïveté by saying things to make me think that I wanted to go further in our relationship instead of waiting until I was ready. Twice I almost made the choice to give in to my emotions before much saner thoughts brought me back to my senses. Then Gary would say things that would reverse the normal roles of a guy and girl by making me feel guilty for tempting him to have sex with me! But with time and a new focus, I made up my mind that I wouldn't do anything that I didn't want to do whether it was with Gary or any other guy.

# Chapter Nine

Lisa insisted that I allow Denise to play an active role in my wedding. Sasha was one of the other bridesmaids along with three of my cousins on my mother's side of the family. I didn't want Denise in my wedding. Our friendship had become strained to the point where I hardly spoke to her. Since I agreed to Lisa's request, I had to bite back my true feelings and smile when I saw her. Not that I didn't still care about Denise, it's just that I'd lost a lot of respect for her because of how she carried herself when she was dealing with Johnny Haines. If she hadn't been so judgmental when it came to the rest of us, and our decisions, especially when it came to guys, I wouldn't have distanced myself from her. Up until college, she was the voice of reason and logic, that great thing called common sense along with wisdom and well-thought out decisions. Only she forgot to include herself in all of this.

While we were getting ready for the wedding, I had little contact with Denise, even when Lisa came into town. During the rehearsals, one of my cousins filled in my place to stand at the altar with Gary because everyone said it was bad luck for the bride to stand there. I hardly spoke to her. Any conversation dealt with her son Amir, her father, or something general enough so that we wouldn't have to talk for too long.

Lisa made reservations at an elegant soul food restaurant called *Kara's*. The place opened six years ago, in the downtown area, and I had been there a few times. I agreed with Lisa that I should spend time with my single friends for the last time before I got married. The four of us were to meet for our eight o'clock reservations the Thursday night before my wedding. Lisa kept up with her Maid of Honor duties by making sure we were at the restaurant no later than seven-fifty. I knew we would have to wait on Sasha since she was usually late. Denise was already there when we walked into the lobby.

As we approached Denise, she gave Lisa a hug and a kiss on her cheek. When our eyes met, I smiled hoping that it would loosen the tight feeling I had in my chest. Reaching my right hand out, I spoke to Denise. She walked toward me, past my hand and hugged me, whispering in my ear that she really misses the friend she had in me. I wasn't expecting that and couldn't come up with a reply. In the meantime Lisa confirmed our reservation with the maître d', and we were immediately taken to our table, one situated in the back of the restaurant, giving us some privacy. By the time we were seated, Sasha came rushing in making apologies for being a little late.

It didn't take us long to start reminiscing about old times and talking about what we were involved in now. Sasha was a paralegal for a firm in the downtown area, deciding that it would take too much of her time to become a lawyer. She did get to sit in on some high profile crime trials, and enjoyed helping the lawyer to prepare his cases. Sasha had gone back to her short haircut, and her hair had started to take on a totally different texture. She no longer needed perms because her hair was that of a newborn baby's. Soft and curly and, as she put it, *a very low maintenance hairdo*. Sasha's skin was still clear and pretty, and she maintained the weight she gained while she was away at college. Her relationship with Quadir was off and on, but for the most part, they were still close. No one asked Sasha anything specific about her condition, and since she looked so healthy, there was no need to bring it up.

Lisa was excited about her plan to rent a small place to begin her fashion design career. When she returned to California after the wedding, she was going to look into it and start by the new year. She had already made a few solid contacts and had designed clothes for a couple of well-known celebrities. Lisa said marrying her fiancé was still way in the future, and having children was even further away. I was hoping she will change some of the styles she created for herself before marriage and children. She had on a hot pink skirt set that hardly had any fabric, revealing more skin then the outfit she wore to my bridal shower. The skirt was up her thighs, and the top she had on revealed her pierced navel. We had a lot to say about that body piercing only to find out she had another one in a well-hidden place, *in the sugar bowl.* We all roared with laughter while some of the patrons stared at us like we were crazy.

After we ordered our food, it was Denise's turn to share. She just started working as an administrative assistant in the Finance department at BAN Technologies, the same company where Gary worked. Gary said that she was very good at the job, had a great eye for detail and was quite innovative and easy to work with. As far as her personal life, ever since she dated Johnny, things haven't been the same in her relationships with guys. She explained that she was, "Single and free and loving every minute of it. The Johnnys in my life are history and I don't feel like getting into a serious relationship with anyone else right now. I can date whoever I want without worrying about sneaking around on somebody else."

"Well, how are Amir and his daddy doing, and is he all right with you seeing other guys?" asked Sasha.

"He knows that we just had a child together and nothing else. We ended up taking a date a little further than either of us intended. So now we have this understanding that we don't have to be together in order for Amir to have a mother and a father, you know?"

When I first walked into the restaurant I made an effort to put my bad feelings about Denise out of my mind, but her last statement made the feeling come back with a vengeance. Her dealings with guys didn't change, and to make matters worse, her son was in the middle of it. Yet she sat there smug in what she was saying, trying to convince the rest of us that it was ok. I couldn't help wondering if this was the new way of handling her relationships with men--have a baby to either keep them or not...I couldn't tell at this point especially considering how she handled things in the past.

I knew this situation was different than when she got pregnant in college, yet it made me have the same feelings that I had during our first year of college.

Denise kept following Johnny to his campus in order to keep the girls away from him. But the harder she tried to make things better between them, the worse things became. Just from what she was telling me, it was clear Johnny wasn't innocent in any of it. Johnny would have a girl in his room when he knew that Denise might show up at any time. Each time Denise would go to his dorm and find him with a different girl, the best explanation he could come up with was that they were just friends. Denise would start acting out, trying to fight the girl, and then end up in Johnny's bed before it was all over with. But by then Denise was pregnant, and she thought keeping the baby would ensure that Johnny would be in her life even if he didn't want to be. I knew she was mistaken because Johnny was already doing what he wanted to do.

I tried to be a good friend to Denise and be there for the times she needed someone to talk to because her father was going to have a fit once he found out about her pregnancy. She claimed to be doing well, but I couldn't understand how when she did not get any prenatal care. Instead she was too busy trying to keep up with Johnny. No amount of coaxing on my part convinced her that she needed to see a doctor for herself and her baby.

A few weeks before spring break our freshman year, Denise called to ask me to ride with her out to Johnny's school on the bus. She didn't have a car yet and had been traveling by bus quite a bit. So, I drove to Trenton. Throughout the drive Denise complained about Johnny and his lack of attention and careless attitude concerning their baby. I regretted my decision to go with Denise and couldn't wait to get to the campus just so I could hear someone else talk.

As we parked in the parking lot outside of Johnny's dorm, Denise spotted Johnny walking towards us with his arm around a girl in a cheerleader outfit. She jumped from the car and was all up in the girl's face before I could collect myself and get out of the car. By the time I reached them, Johnny was holding Denise back while trying to keep the girl from hitting her at the same time. Denise had already started to scream like she had lost her mind while some other students who were outside started to walk toward the direction of the screams.

"Denise! Denise! Stop acting like this in front of these people!" I screamed so she could hear me.

Someone in the crowd said, "Please, this is a show every weekend. Let her get it out of her system." A few more people added their comments, but no one moved to help break up the pending fight. I grabbed Denise by her arms and told her a few times to calm down before campus security arrested us. She stopped screaming, but she didn't stop trying to hit the girl, so Johnny picked her up and took her to his dorm while I trailed behind them. The crowd was murmuring that their weekend entertainment was messed up, and I was more than embarrassed to be there.

Other than Denise's screams, the small campus was quiet. The dorms were within walking distance of the main building of the college. Each dorm building was named after a president and had two floors, and from what I could tell as we passed rooms with open doors, all of the rooms were the same. Two twin beds, two dressers, two desks side-by-side and a closet with double sliding doors. The restrooms and showers were at the end of the hallway. I heard TVs and radios blaring, saw students fooling around in the hallways, and they were watching as Johnny carried Denise into his room, not putting her down until he got into the room. I almost didn't go in because as soon as the door opened, a strong smell of dirty socks hit me, but it was obvious neither Johnny nor Denise were embarrassed. Clothes were all over the floor, empty soda cans and food containers, pizza and Chinese food, were scattered on the desk, and they appeared to have been there for days.

Denise sat on Johnny's bed and crossed her arms and legs as if waiting for Johnny to say something. When he didn't, she started cursing and telling him how she was tired of coming up there to find him with another girl and that they are going to have to come to a decision about their relationship.

"First of all, don't curse at me. I have been telling you for weeks that it's over. You thought having my baby was going to keep me? Think again! I am on full scholarship here to play ball, and nothing you do is going to mess up my chances to go pro, nothing!" Johnny said, moving to stand in front of Denise.

When the tears started to stream down her face, Denise said she had to use the bathroom before we left. There was nothing for me to say to Johnny because it wasn't my business. Ten minutes passed and Denise was still in the bathroom, so I got up to see about her. Denise was sitting on one of the toilets, but the door was locked. I called out to her and when she didn't answer, I went back to the room to get Johnny. He took out a pocketknife, as if he was expecting to have to jimmy the door open. Denise was sitting on the bowl, blood on the inside of her thighs and tears streaming down her face. I started freaking out, running for the phone to call 911. Johnny and I helped to get Denise cleaned up as we waited on the ambulance.

Johnny rode with Denise in the ambulance and I followed in my car, my mind racing from one thought to another, Did Denise do something to abort the baby? Did she lose it because she didn't get prenatal care? But if she did something, what did she use? There was nothing in the bathroom she could have used, or was there?

By the time we reached the hospital, my head ached from going back and forth trying to make this situation make some sense. I sat in the waiting room until Johnny came from Denise's examining room to tell me that Denise lost the baby. He looked sad yet relieved; I felt numb.

"How did she lose the baby? I just don't understand..." I said, looking up at Johnny.

"Tonya, Denise has known for a long time we had nothing to hold on to each other for. I don't want to date just one girl and she thought getting pregnant would change that. It just complicated things, and now she went and...she aborted the baby herself."

"Is that what the doctor is saying? That she actually did that to herself?"

"Yeah, but she's going to be ok. She was about four months along or so...or either she lied to me about how far along she really was. They had to take her for some minor surgery to clean her out or something."

I just sat there wondering if I should bother to call Denise's father, my parents or just what should I do. Then it dawned on me that I didn't know my way home because I paid very little attention as I drove, taking the turns and exits according to Denise's directions. I decided then that I had to call her father and my parents to let them know what happened. What a night that turned out to be. Denise lost her baby, Johnny cared but not enough to stay with her, and Denise's father looked sadder than I'd ever seen him look. All Denise could say is that since there could be no Johnny in her life, there wasn't going to be a connection either, so she had to get rid of the baby. But the baby was also a part of her, and I know that I would have helped as much as I could. I would have definitely supported her decision to keep her baby, and certainly the law would have made Johnny fulfill his financial obligation even if he didn't want to be a part of their lives. But it was already too late to tell Denise my thoughts.

A few years after all of this drama, she got pregnant and had a baby with a guy she never had a real relationship with. My head started reeling again then my friends' laughter brought my attention back to the table and their conversation.

"Denise, you have no sense!" Sasha said. "I wouldn't put up with your mess, huh Tonya?"

"Right…look, I'm ready to go. I still have quite a bit to do before Saturday," I said, not looking at any of them.

Our waitress appeared at this moment asking if we would like some dessert, but we all declined. After placing the check on the table, the waitress walked away and Lisa picked it up, taking out her credit card to pay the bill. I grabbed up my purse, excused myself and headed to the bathroom to freshen myself. When I came out of the stall, Denise was standing next to the sink waiting for me.

"Tonya, what's wrong? I thought dinner was nice and we were having fun like old times, but…"

"But some things never change, Denise. They never change," I said, cutting her off. "Even if they seem to have changed, it's only the flipside of things, no real change."

"I thought being in your wedding and having a chance to talk to you again would heal our friendship...maybe I shouldn't have agreed to be in your wedding."

"Denise, I want you to be in my wedding. Look, maybe I need to accept you for who you are, whether I agree with your choices or whatever. I'll try hard to do that."

"Why wouldn't you do that anyway? Okay, so I've made some bad choices, but I don't regret the fact that I have my son and that there is nothing between me and his father. What is the real reason you are so distant? Does this have to do with me not really being there for you after your attack?"

"No, it doesn't. Well, maybe in part, but that's not the real reason. It's just that ever since your relationship with Johnny didn't work out, you have moved from one guy to the next, and you talk about the sex you had with these guys like it's nothing and..."

"And maybe it isn't! Johnny was my first real boyfriend, Tonya. I haven't been able to stay in a relationship since him, and I really don't want to. Amir was a mistake, but I would never tell my son that because I love him. I admit that I've allowed one bad experience to effect every decision I make about guys, but it's the only way I feel I can guard my heart. If I make light of it, it's because I don't want my true feelings to show," Denise explained, tears filling her eyes.

There was nothing I could say although I understood what Denise was saying to a degree. After a few minutes of awkward silence, I walked out of the ladies' room leaving Denise there to deal with what I wasn't ready to.

# Chapter Ten

Out of sight and out of mind, along with a change of scenery, associates and so-called friends were definitely factors in my decision to forego my alleged singing career. I wanted to be a singer since I was about eight years old. I would spend a lot of time singing in my bedroom mirror with a comb, brush or pencil as my microphone, practicing the songs I would sing, and how I would respond to my many fans. All those dreams of singing and watching the reaction of the people in the audience, and how my voice and the words I would sing changed their lives for the better. I could hear their cheers and requests for encores of the life-changing music. I would take my bow and then arch my hands together in my prayerful thanks to God for making it all possible. Then I would blow kisses to my fans as I exited the stage, smiling as roses were being flung onto the stage.

These thoughts came back to me after I got home from dinner with my friends. The conversation I had with Denise in the bathroom brought back a lot of old memories, good and bad. Singing in the Children's Choir and finding out I could carry a note, then advancing to the Teen Choir where I had an opportunity to sing songs that brought out my true soprano range, and finally the Young Adult Choir where I helped our Directress to teach our new songs and help other choir members with their notes.

This lifelong dream was gone completely after my attack. After my second surgery, I returned to school, part time at a different college. There were no music classes, no voice training classes, nothing remotely close to music of any kind. Instead I changed my major to Early Childhood Education. I put in a lot of time studying and excelled in my studies. Since I no longer sang, to fill in those empty hours left, I got more involved in the ministries at church to avoid the possibility of making new friends at school. It was my way to avoid ending up in a situation similar to the one at my old college.

My parents agreed with the choices I made for school, but they wanted me to talk about what happened to me, even share it with the teens in the Youth Department who would soon be going to college. My father said I could tell them what to watch out for in case they found themselves in a similar situation. It was hard enough thinking about it, much less talking to someone about it. I had testified about it briefly during the revival, and I figured that was enough. Everyone who was close to me knew that subject was off limits.

My special love was working with the young people in the Youth Department. I worked only with the teenage girls, while Tracy Jones worked with all the other youths, and youth leaders. Years ago, if someone told me that I would be working with Tracy, I would not have believed them. When we were growing up, he was too proper and too much of a *good boy*, always being praised by the other parents in the church for knowing how to carry himself and for his maturity. He was too quiet for me and the few times I did talk to him, he acted as if he didn't know what to say. But as he grew into an adult, the way the girls our age looked at him changed almost as quickly as his voice. He was no longer skinny, grew to six feet even, kept his mustache and beard neatly trimmed and wore very nice suits. He always had a smile and a helping hand. Although Tracy received a lot of attention from the girls, he remained respectful and dated only one girl during his last two years of high school.

One Saturday after an outing in the park, Tracy and I went back to the church to put the sport equipment away in the youth office. It was a week before the start of the summer semester. I was set to take a few classes to make up for the semester I missed after the attack. Just as I was about to go, Tracy asked if he could have a few minutes of my time.

"Sure, what's on your mind?" I asked him while placing the file I held in my hand into my brief case.

"First let me ask you how do you like working with the young people? It seems like you're loving it, but if you want to take a different age group, just say the word..."

"Oh no, I really do love it! What I enjoy the most is being able to talk to the young girls who may not be able to talk to their own mother. I don't know if I told you, but I allow them to call me at home if they need to talk on a day other than when we meet. Sometimes they want to discuss things in private and I want to be available to them for that," I explained, closing my brief case. For some reason, I started to feel a little uneasy being alone with Tracy.

"Well, I'm glad to hear that, I really am. But listen, the reason I wanted to talk to you is to ask you if you would like to accompany me to dinner and a movie sometime. Whenever you're available," Tracy said, moving a little closer to me.

I couldn't answer because I was shocked. I had no idea he was attracted to me in that way, especially since we'd been in the same church all of our lives. What I knew about him were all good things; he is a minister in our church, a very serious *churchman* and has organized one of the best youth department outreach ministries in our city. Overall, he is a very nice guy, but I just didn't know why he would wait all these years to show an interest. There were times we would talk, especially during church picnics. Other than that, I never considered Tracy anything more than a friend, and not even a good one. Now that we are both adults, him perhaps more than me since he was twenty-six and had me by three years. I couldn't understand the sudden interest. Just when I'd gotten my thoughts together to give Tracy an answer, Nicole bust through the office door without knocking and plopped down in a chair, arms folded and her lips poked out. Tracy and I looked at each other and then I spoke to Nicole.

"Nicole, what's the matter? You look like you're ready to fight." I moved close to her.

"There is going to be a fight when I catch that girl I saw with my boyfriend!" Nicole rolled her eyes.

"Do you want to talk about it?"

"Not with *him* here..." she answered, her bottom lip beginning to tremble.

"I'm leaving now." Tracy grabbed his briefcase and headed for the door. "Tonya, I'll talk to you tomorrow."

After being out in the sun all day, I was tired and didn't really feel up to fighting with Nicole's nasty attitude. But I had just told Tracy I wanted to be available at times like this, so I had to do it.

"You know that girl that just joined our group, right? When we were leaving the park, she was all up in Chris's face like she go with him," explained Nicole.

"What was Chris doing?" I asked, trying to get some leverage in the situation.

"He was smiling like he liked it! I'm gettin' tired of him disrespecting me like that. Every time some cute girl comes along, he acts like we don't have anything going on."

"What do you think you should do about it, Nicole?"

"I'mma leave him alone, but I'mma get that girl, you watch, I'mma..."

"Whoa wait!" I said, cutting off Nicole's roll. "If you're going to leave Chris alone, do you think it will make any sense to fight the girl? Another thing you should think about is the fact that you are only seventeen years old. Why are you trying to have a committed relationship with anybody? You should be thinking about school and what you're going to do once you graduate high school. You can have male friends, Nicole, but you shouldn't have that kind of relationship with them." I thought Nicole had learned her lesson when the last boyfriend she had tried to hurt her, but I didn't think it was the right time to bring that up.

"But Tonya, I know I love him and he loves me. Chris tells me all the time, and I bet you when I get home tonight he's gonna be calling me and apologizing all hard. So what do I do if he calls?"

"Just what you said a minute ago; that you're going to leave him alone. If he is making you this unhappy, it can't be worth all the apologies he's been feeding you."

"I know why he's treating me this way, so I might as well leave him alone anyway," Nicole said, dropping her head.

Nicole didn't have to tell me because I knew she had sex with her boyfriend. I figured it out because all she could talk about is her boyfriend. I couldn't help wondering where her mother was with this entire situation going on. I pulled her into a hug and told her that I was praying for her and that things were going to be better. I drove Nicole to her house that night, but I continued to worry about her as I drove home and for the rest of the night.

When I woke up the next morning, my thoughts were still on Nicole, wondering if I had handled her situation correctly. Since Gary had transferred to the same college I attended, he was available to be my sounding board on situations close to me like Nicole. I called him so we could get together. The transfer made it possible for him to work part time at the company sponsoring his internship. Being friends with Gary was different because he had received salvation a year ago when the evangelist from Texas was at our church. Later that year, he joined our church, becoming actively involved with the young men's ministry, going to detention homes for under-aged offenders, hospitals, nursing homes or standing on street corners passing out Christian literature. Gary also attempted to keep things going between us as well, but I was very content in focusing on my work in the church and finishing school. He would ask me out to dinner, to the movies or a trip into New York, but I would turn him down before he could finish getting the words out of his mouth.

Every Sunday after church, Gary came over my house for dinner. Afterward he would join my father in the den to watch whatever sporting event happened to be on. He had become a permanent fixture in my family, and I still considered Gary just a very good friend. I still had feelings for him and believed I always would, and he made it a point to let me know that his love for me was stronger and growing every day. We were only twenty-three. I felt we still had at least another five years to think about committing to a serious relationship.

One Sunday, after my parents went up to bed, Gary stayed with me in the den. We didn't talk much because we were watching television, but then right in the middle of a good show, Gary clicked the set off.

"Did you bump your head or something? I was watching that."

"Tonya, can we talk?"

"About what?" I asked, trying to take the remote control from Gary's hand.

"What are we going to do? We've been friends long enough to begin to build on it, don't you think?"

"The fact that we're still good friends is enough, and as far as I'm concerned, we have been building on it. My focus is still on completing school and working with the youth. That is not about to change," I said, crossing my arms.

"Yes, but we've been through enough together and we've been with each other long enough to know what we want...at least I know what I want. Why shouldn't we go to the next level in our relationship?" Gary asked, pulling me to him.

"Let me get through this last semester of school and we can talk about it then. Right now my decision still stands," I said, pulling away from Gary.

Reaching into his shirt pocket, Gary pulled out a ring box and said, "Hold on to this. When you're sure about what you want to do, you can either give it back or put it on."

Gary left without saying another word, and I stood there unable to say anything to stop him from leaving. I knew Gary well, and although he had received salvation and he didn't joke around as much as he used to, he still had a tendency to play mind games, so I let him. Or maybe it's reverse psychology or something because Gary always tried to make me feel guilty about my decisions concerning us, and the next thing I knew, I was doing exactly what I didn't want to do. I just thought the mind games would have ceased by now. But obviously, he felt he still had to use them when it came to me. Gary went home and I went to my room, placing the ring in the top drawer of my desk, but not before I looked at it. I felt my jaw when it dropped because the rock in the ring was huge! It had to be at least a half-carat, but I couldn't think about committing to Gary at that time. I was still trying to come to terms with my feelings and how I viewed myself as a person. Since I was still unsure about myself, there was no way I could bring those doubts into a committed relationship.

The sad part about all of this was that it was almost a repeat of the same conversation we had up at The Hill before the attack. Gary must have thought I had not matured at all or still felt that I couldn't control my emotions when it came to him. Being in love with him was one thing, but I knew in my heart that I wasn't ready to commit to him. I still had some growing to do, some soul searching to do, and all these insecurities would cause problems in a relationship.

Over the next four weeks, he started to woo me, taking me to dinner, movies, long drives or anything else he could think of, to convince me to consider his marriage proposal. But I never took the ring out of the box to even try it on, and his patience wore thin one evening while we were sitting up at The Hill.

"How can you sit there and not agree that things are perfect for us to come together? Don't you like the ring? I have a good job and I can take care of you and give you anything you want, Tonya. Why don't you want this?"

"Do I have to keep explaining things to you, Gary? This is just not the right time for me, ok? We're right back where we have always been…first you're interested and I'm not, then I am and you're not…"

"Are you trying to tell me that you don't love me anymore, Tonya?" Gary asked, cutting me off. "Because if that's what you're trying to say…"

"No, that's not what I'm saying! I do love you, it's just that I feel rushed and I don't want to do anything when I feel like I'm being forced to do it. You just have to give me some more time. Please? A little more time…" I began to feel like I was doing something wrong to Gary.

Instead of answering me, Gary started the car and headed back towards town and my house. Since neither of us spoke a word, feelings of guilt began to ride me, but I reasoned with myself that there was no cause for that. I was finally at a place in my life where I felt comfortable making my own decisions and I wasn't going to allow Gary or anyone else to *make* me do something I knew I wasn't ready to do. Then I started to get angry thinking that Gary had a lot of nerve trying to force himself and a relationship on me. He should know better than anyone else that it just wasn't the right time. The closer we got to my house, the angrier I became because I felt Gary was taking advantage of my feelings.

When we arrived at my house, Gary walked me to the door and asked for his ring back! I knew it was another mind game, but by now I was angry. I stomped up the stairs. When I returned downstairs, I practically threw the ring in his face. Gary put his hand up just in time to catch it before it hit him. It would have stung him pretty good since I flung it with all my might.

"Just like that? You're not gonna put up a fight to keep it?" Gary asked, as if he was surprised by my actions and attitude.

"Why should I? You're asking for it back." I didn't even look at him.

Thinking that just this once I would beat Gary at his own game, but I was the one surprised when Gary took the ring and left that night. We barely spoke to each other after that, and when the relationship ended, so did Gary's Sunday afternoon visits for dinner. When he did this, I had to tell my parents what was really going on, *after* he provided them with his version of things. My parents kept their comments to a minimum, and plans for school and working with the young people at church continued. I still had half of the summer semester to finish in order to graduate. So I pushed thoughts of Gary and his proposal to the back of my mind.

Without Gary around, I had more time for the youths in my group. That also made me more available for Tracy. He took advantage of the times we were together to talk to me once he found out that things didn't work out between me and Gary. After a month of refusing to go out with him, I decided to take Tracy up on a date to dinner and a movie. I reasoned it wouldn't hurt anybody, and if I didn't enjoy myself, it would be our very last date. At least that was what I told myself, but after I agreed to the date, I was filled with regret.

Trying to view Tracy as a real date was difficult because I found myself comparing him to Gary. Gary knew me better, what I liked to eat, my favorite color, what to say to make me laugh, and Tracy...well, he knew me from church and working with the young people, but did he really want to know me on a personal level? Trying to mix personal with ministry was something I had not considered before and needed to think out thoroughly before I allowed anything other than friendship to grow between me and Tracy.

There were only a few days left before my first date with Tracy. It had been a month since Gary and I stopped talking. I couldn't decide whether to cancel the date or cut it short. On the one hand, going out with Tracy didn't mean we couldn't remain the friends we had always been. Yet, I felt like I was cheating on Gary. I even thought about calling Gary to see how he felt about me going out on a date with another guy but realized how stupid that thought was and changed my mind. Finally after weighing all of my options, there was no real reason to back out at the last minute, but I made up my mind that there would not be another date.

On date night, I felt there was still a chance of things working out with Gary. I couldn't deny that I missed Gary coming around. I got ready, hoping that it would be well worth my time. Since Tracy and I never discussed anything other than youth department activities and plans, we rode in silence in Tracy's father's dark blue Acura Legend. Tracy's old beat up Honda Accord was in the shop. It was a nice night, not too hot, so Tracy had the back passenger windows halfway down with the vent on low. I found myself watching what people were doing outside my window instead of trying to make conversation with Tracy.

We went to Kara's. It was my first time since they redecorated it, to off-white, dark green, light green and touches of gold carpet; tablecloths to match the carpet and evenly distributed throughout with decorative real floral arrangements at each table or booth. The lights were down low and jazz music played softly and inviting through their speaker system. The waiter led us to an almost secluded booth. I guess he thought we wanted to be alone. I wanted a table in the middle of the floor. If only I could think of an excuse to go home or find some way to speed this evening up because we still didn't have much to talk about, and I was feeling a little uncomfortable.

"How's the teaching job going?" Tracy asked in an attempt to get some kind of dialogue going between us.

"It's going just fine. I enjoy the children more than I thought I would. I'm going to miss them when I have to leave."

"Why are you leaving?" He sounded concerned.

"I'm a substitute teacher. My assignment ends after Thanksgiving when their teacher returns. I'm hoping a position opens up for me soon. If you don't mind me asking, what do you do?"

"I'm an accountant. Love working with numbers and balancing other folks' bank accounts," Tracy said with just a hint of a smile on his face as if he was amused that I showed an interest.

"A rewarding job."

"It has its ups and downs, but basically I enjoy it."

We talked through dinner and chatted some on the way to see "Nutty Professor", starring Eddie Murphy. The movie is what helped me begin to feel comfortable with Tracy. When a real funny part came on, I would pound on Tracy's shoulder with my fist when I couldn't catch my breath! We even shared a box of buttered popcorn. By the end of the evening, I was glad I went out with him. The date didn't turn out as boring as I thought it would, and it was really good to get out of the house and do something.

On the way home we didn't really have much to talk about. Tracy was sweet and all and insisted he open the car door for me. Then taking my hand, Tracy walked me up the stairs and we sat on the porch for a little while since the night wasn't really cold. We didn't say anything at first, but Tracy spoke up to ease the awkward feeling that started to settle between us.

"I've never heard you laugh like that before," Tracy said while leaning on the back of one of the chairs on the porch of my house.

"Eddie does it to me every time," I said, remembering the movie. "I just love Eddie to death! The critics once said that Eddie was washed up and couldn't make a come back. That's all right because he'll always be funny to me."

I began to feel uncomfortable because I knew talking about the movie wouldn't last. He was bound to try to get personal, and it was the last thing I wanted.

"Hope we can go to Eddie's next movie together," Tracy said while reaching over to stroke my chin.

"Maybe..." was all I could come up with.

"As long as it's not five years from now, huh?" Tracy said with a smile, grabbing me by both hands. "That way we can share the movie together sooner..."

We laughed, feeling awkward once again since the evening had come to an end and there was really nothing left to say.

"I'd better go inside. Saturday is a big day in our house." Tracy took my hand in his and kissed it softly. I really didn't want to get into anyone else, but he was so sweet! "Tracy, I really did have a good time."

"I'm glad."

I gave Tracy a quick hug and dashed into the house and to bed, not even considering if I would even continue to date Tracy, which I did, only I felt we were just meeting as friends, or to discuss a Youth Department issues. Then we started going out at least once a week for dinner and a movie, but when he started coming on a little too strong, I had to end things. Obviously for Tracy, the dinners meant that our relationship was growing and eventually he would work his way up from holding my hand to placing his arm around my shoulders, and finally get his first kiss. No matter how many times I made it clear to him that I didn't feel that way about him, he just kept on going as if his process would wear me down. Quite honestly, it wouldn't have ended so soon had we not run into Gary one evening while we were out celebrating my permanent teaching position.

A few weeks before, after church, Gary told me about his promotion and transfer to California. He was out having dinner with a young lady I didn't know, and I immediately became jealous. Gary and I greeted each other coldly. When we did speak, our words were laced with sarcasm. There was no way Tracy didn't pick up on it. Not only that, Gary's table was not too far from ours, and every now and then when Tracy was trying to talk to me, I was busy trying to see what was going on at Gary's table. Tracy followed my gaze to Gary's table and saw that Gary was staring right back at me. By the time we finished eating dinner, I knew that I could not continue going out with Tracy when I still had feelings for Gary.

Gary and his date got up to leave before we did, so he came over to our table to shake hands with Tracy and say a curt, "good night, Tonya." I just said, "whatever" and turned my head the other way, but not before I saw Gary put his hand in the small of the young lady's back as they headed toward the exit. That is when my evening ended. I told Tracy that I had changed my mind about going to the movies. All I wanted to do was go home and curl up in my bed. Tracy didn't try to change my mind. He just paid the check and we left the restaurant.

Tracy and I rode home in silence. When he parked in front of my house, he sat there clenching his teeth, rubbing both of his thumbs over the steering wheel. I could tell he wanted to say something, but I decided to just end the night. I opened my door to go inside of the house without addressing what had happened at dinner. Instead of allowing me to get away, Tracy followed me to the door, took my hand and insisted I tell him if I still had feelings for Gary.

"Maybe we shouldn't go out any more until you're sure of things," Tracy said, sounding defeated.

"I'm sure of my feelings for you and Gary. We, Gary and I, have been fighting against something we've had together for the last four years, and it's not working. So, us not seeing each other anymore is a good idea. I enjoy working with you and the children, but to have something on a personal level is just not working," I said, trying to make sure Tracy understood that I was taking full blame for this mess.

"Okay, Tonya, if that's what you want. I'll see you in church then," Tracy said, slowly releasing my hand.

"Without a doubt. I'll see you Sunday. Goodnight." I kissed Tracy lightly on his lips, unlocked the door and eased in without looking back, at least not until I heard his car door slam. Poor guy, he sat there for about five minutes before he started his engine and pulled away from the curb. I had to admit that I did still have feelings for Gary, but I also knew that I didn't want a serious relationship with Gary or Tracy.

• • •

Two months to the day after Gary and I broke up, he came by my house to tell me he was offered a promotion and would have to move to California. Even though we were no longer seeing each other, my heart sank. I knew once he left, he would find someone who would be willing to be with him. Instead of trying to hear him out, I acted as if I didn't really care. "Why are you telling me this, Gary?"

"So we can come to a definite resolve about us. I'll make my decision based on that. What I feel for you hasn't changed. I thought we would have talked by now, but we could never get together."

"Whatever...anyway..."

"If you are willing to start over with me, I'll stay. If not, I'm outta here."

"If the opportunity is so great, why would you give it up for a relationship with me? I mean, really, Gary," I kept pretending I didn't care.

"Love makes you do the strangest things." Gary looked as if he was being sincere. "Look at you, Tonya. You're so good with children, how could you not want a family of your own?"

"Who says I don't? I just don't want to get married right now. So what's your point?" I asked, wanting to end the conversation.

"I just believe it's time you thought about yourself for a change. It's real good that you touch so many children's lives, and believe me, they will always remember you for it. But what about your life? Maybe you think I'm not the man for you, but I do. I also believe there is something you're not coming to terms with. That's what your problem is."

"Is that right, Mr. Know-it-All? F.Y.I., there is nothing I need to come to terms with!" I said, trying hard not to get angry.

According to Gary, I was hiding behind my ministry, work and other things to avoid having to deal with some emotions I had buried away. He tried to convince me that if I didn't deal with them, they would come up unexpectedly one day and I wouldn't be able to handle them. I couldn't *believe* Gary was taking me there! I started pacing the floor trying to control my anger, but Gary continued to talk. "I know that you were blessed to overcome what happened to you and you went on with your life after what Sam did..."

"That part of my life is over with, and I don't have to relive it!" I said, cutting Gary off.

"Have you come to terms with the emotional side of the attack?" He didn't allow me to change the subject.

"Whatever! I still don't have to deal with it," I said, turning my back to him.

Gary went on to explain that he had learned that no matter what it is, once we come to terms with it, we can go on. Whether it's for the good or the bad. That way, when it's over, it's really over.

Yeah, right! He can stand there and preach to me but he didn't go through what I did. Yet, he was telling me what I needed to do.

"I don't have nightmares any more. I'm not ashamed nor am I afraid to go out in public alone. What more do you want from me?" I was on the verge of tears.

"What really happened to you that night?"

"I don't believe you're asking me this!" I turned to face Gary.

"You said nothing happened other than the beating. I think mentally and emotionally that it took something away from you."

I didn't want to admit that I felt like I was raped, that part of me was left on the floor of the auditorium and I didn't know how to get it back. This was the part of the attack I kept hidden, so I wouldn't have to feel the pain or the shame of being violated, of being touched against my will. I knew that one day I would have to deal with it, but this wasn't the day.

"What could that possibly be?" I demanded.

"The part of you that wants to share herself with a man. If you notice, it's easy for you to have female friends, but with guys, you get to a point and back up. You don't know..."

"I don't know how to be in a relationship with a guy, okay? I don't think I'll ever be able to function as a wife..."

"So you run from it when it gets too close. That's why I said that maybe you should have counseling. You can go to Pastor for that," Gary said, softening his voice.

"I'm just really scared, that's all. I'll be okay with a little more time..."

Gary took my hands and held them in his, pleading with me with his eyes. I tried to look away, but he turned my face back to him.

"I know I've acted almost crazy when it comes to you, but I want to be able to tuck our children in bed with you. I want to spend the rest of my life with you."

"Gary..."

"Don't say anything. If you really don't want this, when I walk out that door, I'm gone for good. The choice is yours."

Facing Gary, I knew that I loved him so much. I'd never met anyone that I loved more, but I couldn't trust what we have to come together? In my heart, I sincerely believed that he was the one for me, but I couldn't bring myself to say the words. Gary turned my hands loose, kissed me on my cheek and headed out the door. I just couldn't bring myself to tell him I wanted the same things that he wanted.

• • •

From that day, I realized the last thing I wanted to do was make any major decisions in my life. I wanted everything that was going on in my life to have a smooth transition, so I could finally feel like I had a little control over what I did. I was offered the permanent teaching job around the same time I graduated from college, so I had two things to celebrate. I wouldn't actually be teaching on a permanent basis until the coming September. My parents decided that they would throw me a small celebration party, at the house, to share my blessings with relatives, church family and my friends.

Though I had bottled it up for nearly a year, I missed Gary and wished he could be here. Feelings of regret filled me, but I fought them off and finished getting ready. I wore an off-white, short-sleeved casual dress with a pair of light brown sandals, put a few drops of Poison cologne behind my ears, on my neck and on each thigh, and then headed for the kitchen to help my mother.

My mother and I finished preparing the food to take out to the backyard just as the doorbell rang announcing the arrival of our first guests. I wasn't surprised to see my mother's parents standing on the porch. I escorted them to the backyard. We had set up every lawn chair we owned. My father had already fired up the grill and was just putting the hotdogs and hamburgers on. It wasn't long before the backyard was filled with happy voices and laughter. Relatives and friends were engaged in conversation while the younger children played volleyball at the far end of the yard. Lisa was able to attend because it was July, but it seemed she was there to keep my male cousins occupied, flirting with them and walking past them frequently to show off her white mini skirt and light blue halter top that showed plenty of cleavage. Sasha sat close to Quadir to keep away any advances from the guys. She never did date other guys, and because she is pretty, she felt protected by her relationship with Quadir. Tracy was also invited but he begged off saying he had a previous engagement for the same day.

Everything was going well, the food and barbeque was excellent and there were a lot of stories being told. I looked up and saw Denise coming around the house just as I was about to open my gifts. We had a falling out, so I was quite surprised that she would bother to come. It was no ordinary disagreement, but an all out argument. In the past we never stayed angry more than a day, but this time, I'd been refusing any of her phone calls and didn't return any of them.

Denise came over and handed me a gift, kissing me on my cheek as if everything was cool between us. I thanked her and continued with the festivities, eating and laughing with my guests, hoping that if I didn't talk to her, she would catch the hint and leave. Unfortunately she didn't and decided to stay after everything was over to help us clean up. I still tried to avoid talking to Denise, but it seemed everywhere I turned, there she was. When I told her I was going up to my room, she asked if she could come along because she needed to tell me something. I started to make excuses, but when Denise kept insisting, I invited her in.

"Okay, Denise, what is it? I'm about to take a long bath and call it a night."

"Did you know that Gary was back in town? I saw him at the mall today with some girl that came home with him."

"Is that what he told you?" I asked, my heart racing at the mention of Gary's name.

"That's how he introduced her. He said she's a coworker, but she was leaning on his shoulder while they were looking at some jewelry, and I figure no one is going to do that out in public if it's not more to it than that."

"What would you know about something like that when you're like that with all the guys you get with? Gary and I are not together anyway, so..."

"Hold up! Don't try to make this seem like it's about me. We went there a few weeks ago and I'm not going to argue with you again about my lifestyle, Tonya."

"You know what, Denise? I think you would do well to just mind your business. You're the last person I would take any advice from when it comes to guys. You don't know Gary like I do, and I know he wouldn't bring some girl home to flaunt in my face..."

"You have always been so naïve, Tonya," Denise said with a smirk on her face.

That was it! I asked Denise to please leave my house. As far as I was concerned, when the door closed behind her, so did the door on our friendship. After she left, I tried hard not to entertain what she had said about Gary. I began to pace the room, and felt like the walls were closing in on me. When I couldn't stand it any longer, I slipped out of the front door and started driving, heading in no particular direction.

I drove around and just cried. My tears blurred the headlights from the other cars, the white lines in the road all ran together, and my head started pounding relentlessly, further obscuring my thoughts. I had no idea what time it was when I left the house, and when I finally checked the time, it was well past three in the morning. I was sitting up at The

Hill, and all I could do was think about what I had with Gary and what I still wanted. The Hill was the last place for me to be. It brought back too many memories. Between the tears and the confused thoughts, I had no idea what I was going to do or how I would handle myself with Gary. It seemed that I really didn't have any choice in the matter since it appeared that Gary had already made a decision for the both of us.

I can't remember when I fell asleep, but it took me a few minutes to figure out why I was in my car as the sun beckoned the start of a new day. A cloud seemed to be sitting on me, keeping the warmth from the sun's rays away from me. Knowing my parents would be worried about me, I used my cell phone to call my house. I'd already decided not to go to church that morning.

My parents did a lot of pleading with me to come home, letting me know my grandparents had stayed over and how everyone was concerned about me. But going home was far from my mind. All my parents would do is try to smother me with their love and advice, but this time it was going to be different. The last thing I wanted to do was talk to them.

When we ended the call, I decided to head to the local Holiday Inn. I checked in, paying for three nights. All I needed was time to begin some personal healing. I shut myself in my room, only going out once to buy a few outfits to have a change of clothes. By the third day, I felt like I was going crazy, and searching for a need to feel like my mind wasn't gone, I called home believing the familiar might just put things on track.

After hanging up with my parents, my depression sunk into my bones and sent me into a fit of deep sobs, reminding me of how I felt after being attacked by Sam. I sat in the room and cried. I tried to think things through and how I would be able to accept that Gary actually had someone new in his life. I even thought that Denise may have been mistaken about what she saw, or even lied to get back at me for the harsh words I said to her in our last argument.

But Gary knew what I had been through, so why would he deliberately hurt me by bringing some girl home, and so soon? It just didn't make much sense to me and the only way to ease my mind and the crazy thoughts was to place a call to Gary.

When Gary didn't answer after three rings, I hung up but then called back to leave a nasty message about his new friend. I knew when I was doing it that I was wrong, but I couldn't help myself. Reminding Gary of his words concerning my so-called problems, I told him a friend would be there for a friend and not lie about their feelings. After hanging up, I got into a hot shower and cried until there was nothing left but dry heaves. I felt like I couldn't go on and decided that the weekend was too soon to go back home. After drying off and moisturizing my body after my shower, I got on my knees beside the bathtub and began to pray:

*"Dear Lord, I need You to completely heal me and to help me come to terms with all that I am facing. I must now be honest with you concerning the way I feel about being attacked by Sam and what I believe is left of me as a person. I have never told a soul, never uttered verbally how I feel, just pushed it way back into my subconscious. Lord, I really love Gary with all my heart but I couldn't even say those very words to him.*

*Yet I thank You for the strength You have restored in me, for giving my life back to me, and the love of God in my heart that has compelled me to go on ,only now I feel I have come to a dead end..."*

Exiting the bathroom, I asked for guidance today, right now, for the help and the strength I needed to get back up again.

• • •

As I was combing my hair out, the front desk called and said I had a visitor. I started to tell them I wasn't expecting anyone, but out of curiosity and the fact that I was lonely, I went down to the lobby hoping maybe it was my father coming to rescue me. But when the elevator doors opened, there stood Gary waiting for me! How in the world did he know where I was? My feet were frozen to the floor, and I couldn't move until I heard the elevator doors close behind me as Gary walked towards me.

"How did you know where I was?" I asked Gary, letting him know I was angry.

"Caller I.D. I called your parents to let them know where you are. They're trying to give you time to work things out. Tonya, are you all right? Your eyes are all puffy and..."

"Why don't you leave, Gary?"

"Because I want to help you, Tonya. I want to be here for you."

We stood there looking at each other, taking in each other's appearance. Gary was dressed in a nice pair of jeans, a comfortable-looking t-shirt and still had his hair in twists, now hanging just off his shoulders. His mustache and beard were neatly trimmed and he had on cologne that I had never known him to wear. Gary looked more mature than he did when I saw him last almost a year ago, and it seemed he had a new quiet strength about him. In an attempt to keep my real emotions hidden, I turned away from Gary and pushed the button for the elevator.

The elevator doors opened and Gary followed me, stepping to the back of the elevator as I pushed the button for my floor. We didn't speak until we were inside the room. That's when Gary launched into this long drawn out thing about my parents being worried about me and that I should go back home. I tuned him out and flipped on the television, only to have him walk over to the set and turn it off again.

"What do you want, Gary? Don't you have someone waiting on you that you should be spending time with?" I knew I sounded real immature.

"I don't know what you're talking about…"

"Denise told me that she saw you with some girl or something at the mall…"

"I figured she would do that. Tonya, she's a co-worker. We're not involved. She just wanted to see the east coast so she caught a flight home with me. Denise told you…" Gary said, beginning to laugh to himself. I didn't see why he found the situation to be funny, so I clicked the television back on to end our conversation. Gary turned it off again and I told him I didn't feel like playing games.

"Tonya, come on and go home…whatever is bothering you, it can be worked out better at home."

"Why don't you just leave? As a matter of fact, get out! I really don't want you here, okay? I'll be fine without you and that is what I prefer. So go!"

Gary walked over to me and took my hand, pulling me off the bed and into his arms. His touch evoked a feeling I had never experienced with him, like he would hurt me and another part of me would be ripped away and lost forever. Suddenly I was back in that auditorium and fear seemed to overwhelm me. I started to struggle to get out of Gary's embrace.

"No, stop, get off me!"

I cried and shrank down to the floor. All the emotions I had bottled up came to the surface. The first one was shame, feeling that people could look at me and see what Sam had done to me. Guilt followed closely behind; guilt because I made the choice to put myself in a position to be attacked, guilt because I should have had better control. Only that wasn't possible. Low self-esteem was an overpowering feeling. As much as I had recently accomplished, I still felt like I was nothing and that all I had done hadn't made a difference. There was no way I should be trying to help the youth because I couldn't help myself. Most of all I felt very ugly, unattractive and dirty, convinced that I couldn't be loved by anyone and worst of all I couldn't return love to a man. I couldn't stand being touched by a man and I still had the fear Sam had caused, that all my relationships would fail.

Gary got down on the floor with me and held me until I stopped crying. He held me tenderly and spoke sweetly into my ear, his voice barely above a whisper. Then I heard what he was saying; he was praying earnestly for me that I be delivered from my fears. All the time I've known Gary, we never prayed together, alone. This act changed so many things in me. I gave in to the prayer that he prayed because that part of my attack for some reason I never let go. We were both blessed of God that night, and rejoiced because I was finally able to surrender all of those emotions to God. Afterwards we hugged one another in genuine love; not the love you have man to woman, but the love of God in our hearts.

We sat up most of the night, talking and getting all of our feelings out in the open. I was able to share all of my fears with Gary, telling him that I wish I wasn't afraid to tell him I didn't want him to go to California, knowing I would have ended up running him away had he decided to stay. And that the break up and all that I went through was a blessing to me because it forced me to come to terms with my real feelings, something Gary told me before he left.

Gary looked at his watch and saw that the hour was far spent and suggested that we get some sleep. I agreed realizing that I was drained emotionally and physically. Gary started to pull the extra sheet from the bed to sleep on the floor, but I insisted he share my bed. I wanted to feel the warmth of his body comforting me as I slept.

I went into the bathroom to undress, taking with me a long t-shirt to change into. After washing my face, brushing my teeth and pulling my hair into a ponytail, I went back into the room. Gary had removed his clothes with the exception of his silk boxers and all I could do was stand there and feel my jaw fall open. He had obviously been working out because his body was toned and a sculpted. The muscles in his chest, stomach, arms, thighs and legs looked like someone drew them perfectly! Soft, slightly curly hair covered Gary's chest and stomach, and I followed the trail until it reached the top of his boxers; it wasn't until then that I felt self-conscious and busied myself with pulling the blanket back on the bed.

"I can put my shirt back on if that will make you feel more comfortable."

"No, I'm ok... really," I hurried to get under the blanket and turn my back to Gary. He climbed in, and I closed my eyes as if that would erase the picture I had of his body in my mind. With my eyes still closed, I inched close enough to Gary for our bodies to touch. When Gary didn't say anything, I got closer.

"Are you sure you're not going to try to seduce me?" Gary joked.

"Only if you want me to," I replied, smiling.

When we finally settled ourselves under the blanket, Gary kissed me softly on my neck. I took his arm and wrapped it around me and snuggled up against him as close as I could.

"Mmmmm... you'd better stop moving back, Tonya," Gary said.

I didn't answer and just enjoyed the feel of Gary's body against mine, the smell of his cologne, and the light breeze from his breath on my neck. I truly loved this man with my whole heart. Just before I dozed off to sleep, I whispered ever so softly, "I love you, Gary."

As soon as I said it, he grabbed my earlobe softly between his teeth and said, "I love you too." His words were a little mumbled because he still held my ear lobe in his teeth, but they still filled my heart with a warmth I can't ever remember feeling. Falling asleep, I remember thinking to myself, so this is what real love feels like...warm, comfortable, sweet...I can get used to this real quick.

I snuggled a little closer to Gary and fell asleep, with a smile on my face to the sound of his even breathing in my ear.

• • •

Gary followed me home the next morning and waited for me to go in the house before he pulled away. My father was livid and my mother was hugging me as if I had been gone for years. We were in the kitchen discussing why I ran away the way I did, but after listening to my father ranting and raving about me up and leaving and him worrying, how it looked after the way I was raised, I couldn't hold back any longer.

"That is the whole problem! You and Mom have always controlled everything I did, everywhere I went, how I am supposed to act and a host of other things. But no more, uh uh, things are going to be different from now on. I don't need you to do that for me anymore. Do you see where it led? It's a wonder I didn't end up in a loony bin somewhere."

"Hold on just one minute, Tonya! Who do you think you're talking to?" my father asked, his eyebrows knitted and his face in a frown.

"Dad, look, I am not being disrespectful, but it's time you realize that you cannot control my life. The reality of it is, you never could, and it took most of my life for me to realize that."

"Is that what you think? That we tried to control your life? Tonya, all we tried to do is…" my mother started to explain.

"Protect me. Yes, I've heard it a million times, Mom, but you can't even do that. The situation with Sam convinced me of that. Granted, it was my decision to be in the singing group, but if you could protect me from everything, being with the group would not have happened either."

We were all quiet for a few minutes. My mother took a sip of her cold cup of tea and seemed to be in deep thought while my father paced in front of the back door. The silence felt like a heavy blanket over us, then my father asked in a quiet voice, "Tonya, are you blaming us for what happened to you that night?"

"I used to, Dad, I really did. But I know now that you didn't purposely make me believe that you could always protect me. It's natural for parents to want to protect their children, but we all have to face the reality that it just isn't possible." The anger I initially felt began to wane.

Out of respect I had always obeyed them, but from that moment on, I felt my future choices should be mine and if I needed or wanted their advice, I would ask. By the time I realized what I had said, both of my parents were speechless. I went up to my room, feeling bad about the way I spoke to my parents. But, they needed to know how I felt and should appreciate the fact I told them.

I stayed up in my room for the rest of the day to avoid looking at my parents and feeling guilty. Yet, it felt good to finally be able to say what I had been thinking for quite some time. I knew once things are said you cannot take them back, and since our words are vehicles of faith, they have an effect and I should have expected a reaction. So for the next few days we were all tiptoeing around each other, trying not to say anything that may offend the other. I couldn't stand this and figured I had to do something to make things better, so I pretended I needed my mother's advice on a few of the youth activities on the list I had been preparing. It worked! And as usual, my mother told my father about it and it helped him feel a little comfortable about talking to me again.

The following week I kept myself busy by working on the youth activities so I wouldn't think about Gary. He was here on vacation, and had a lot of work to do around his mother's house. He had called a few times to explain his distance, so I was a little surprised he stopped by the Saturday before he was to leave for California. The doorbell rang and my mother let him in and he came up to my bedroom. I was sitting at my desk when Gary knocked. There was no need to act surprised because I saw him pull up in front of my house, but I couldn't wipe the big smile off of my face.

"Sorry I am just coming by...it's been crazy with my mother all week. I wanted to come by before today, but my mother took up most of my time," Gary said, kissing me on my cheek as we hugged.

"That's ok. I've been pretty busy myself getting things prepared for the young people at church," I sat on the bed.

We talked about what we've been doing since we last saw each other. I had finished college and accepted a permanent job, teaching first graders. Gary was working long hours, sometimes on Saturday, stabilizing his position in California. We laughed and shared so much that afternoon. It felt really good. We were then silent for long stretches, our backs against the wall, snuggled up while sitting on the bed.

As the hours passed, Gary's stomach growled so I fixed some turkey club sandwiches and grabbed a couple of sodas from the fridge. When I returned, I pulled an old blanket from the closet and spread it on the floor and set the food up on it. When we were through, I started gathering up the plates and cups, but Gary stopped me and asked me to have a seat on my bed. I hesitantly sat down on my bed, my heart beating fast because I just knew he was going to tell me that the best we could be is friends. After the night we spent together at the hotel, although we did nothing but sleep, I thought he would change his mind and give our relationship another chance.

"I have a six o'clock flight out to Cali tomorrow, so that means that I will be leaving right after church, ok? But I want you to know today was really sweet...I enjoyed spending this time with you."

"Yeah..." was all I could say.

"I've got to get my mother's car back to her, but before I go, I need to ask you something," Gary said, lifting my chin up so I could look at him. "Will you be my wife?"

"Wha-what? Are you serious? I mean, you're not just saying that are you, because if you are..." He cut me off by placing his lips over mine. While we kissed, Gary dug into his pocket and pulled out the ring I'd returned. Pulling me off the bed and holding me in his arms he asked again, "Will you be my wife?"

"Yes..." I whispered. Gary then took my left hand, kissed each finger tenderly and finally placed my engagement ring on my left ring finger. I kissed him on his forehead, each eye, his nose, his cheeks and then his lips, opening my mouth to receive his tongue as the tears from my eyes formed a seal around our lips.

Before going downstairs to share the news with my parents, we talked about our plans for the wedding. We both wanted the same things, and each took turns defending the major questions:

"Tonya and I have mutually come to this decision, Mr. Henderson. The timing couldn't be better either since I will be moving back here. Not because of my marriage proposal, but because our company didn't do as well as anticipated out on the West Coast. We're going to cut our losses and have everything cleared out in the next six weeks."

"That should be enough time to plan a wedding. We have set the date for Saturday, August 31."

"But Tonya, it's the third week of July. Are you sure you want to plan a wedding at such short notice?" my mother wanted to know.

"We're sure," I said taking Gary's hand in mine.

I could tell my father was struggling with trying not to take control of things for me. Since my parents knew how I felt about their advice and smothering ways, they held their tongues and kept any negative thoughts to themselves.

• • •

After church the next day, Gary and I said a quick good-bye. I started missing him as soon as his car pulled out of the church parking lot, but I had plenty of things to think about. My mother bought about eight or nine bride magazines. I never knew there was so much to do for a wedding. I had to decide on wedding colors, pick invitations and mail them as soon as possible. Find a reception hall big enough to hold our forever increasing guest list, and then select a menu. Choosing my bridesmaids wasn't hard, but picking out the style for their dresses and my wedding dress wasn't easy. Next we had to reserve blocks of rooms at the local hotel for reservations for family and friends, pick out the favors, and find a good photographer who will also videotape our special day and come up with a theme for the wedding. That was the easiest decision I made while planning the wedding. "One Love" was our theme and our theme song, to be played when the wedding party marches in. The song was by the gospel group Commissioned and their CD, "Time and Seasons." I knew it was the right time and season for Gary and I to become one. To add to the theme, I had small cards printed to be placed at everyone's place setting at the reception with the scripture from Ecclesiastes third chapter, first verse: "To everything there is a *season*, and a *time* to every purpose under the heaven."

August was here before I knew it, and by then I wished I had just eloped or something.

My grandparents and a host of aunts, uncles and cousins on both sides of the family arrived in town as scheduled, and my father couldn't pass up an opportunity to get us all together before the wedding. He fired up the grill, and with the help of a few uncles, we had an unofficial family reunion in our backyard.

Gary arrived a week before the wedding, with his car loaded down with clothes and personal items. He had shipped his furniture and it was set to arrive the week of our wedding.

With the final plans taking most of our time, the eve of the wedding was our first chance to spend quality time together. We went out to dinner and talked about the layout of the wedding as if it was our first time talking about it, ensuring each other that everything was in place and ready to go. We also talked about the things we expected during our marriage other than children and assured each other that the fairy tale myth of "happily ever after" was just that, a myth.

"You know as soon as we get back in town from our honeymoon we're going to have to look for a place of our own," Gary said, taking a sip of his soda.

"I know. Are you sure your mother is okay with us staying at her house? You know my parents wouldn't mind if we stayed at my house."

"It's cool, don't even worry about it. Listen, I need to tell you something about me. It's something you should know before tomorrow."

"Okay, I'm listening."

"I have never had sex before…"

My jaw dropped and a piece of the cake I just put in my mouth fell back into my plate! "Wait a minute…you always dated in high school and you're sitting here telling me that you never?" I asked, wiping my mouth with my napkin.

"I was the biggest perpetrator in high school. I learned how to kiss and feel on girls early, and made an art of it, but I never felt comfortable enough with a girl to go that far. When things started to get a little too hot, I would find a way to break things off," Gary explained, as if it was a normal thing.

I may have been raised that way and believe that way, but I never thought it would be possible to marry a man who was chaste. A feeling of relief flooded me because we would learn how to make love together equally, and I no longer felt inadequate compared to Gary, thinking that I wouldn't measure up to all the other girls he'd been with.

Gary drove me home, and we sat on the porch talking until about eleven o'clock. I got up from the chair and stretched, and told Gary it was time for him to leave since it was supposed to be bad luck for the groom to see the bride the day of the wedding.

"Are you sure you're ready to do this?" Gary asked me, standing and pulling me into a tight hug.

"If I'm not, it's too late to turn back now," I said, burying my head into his chest.

"Don't come to that altar tomorrow and say you're not ready or I'm going off in that church," Gary said, trying to make a joke of it, but I knew he was serious.

I reached up and kissed his lips, hugged him again and made my way into the house. Before preparing for bed, I looked at my wedding dress and the accessories, trying to imagine my wedding day. I knew it was something I wanted to do, but I still had feelings of doubt and uncertainty. I couldn't fall asleep and was up well past two in the morning. As I searched for something to occupy my time, I heard a light knock on my door. My mother asked if she could come in and I welcomed her presence, immediately feeling at ease.

In spite of what I'd told my parents about not wanting their advice, I longed to hear my mother's comforting words, and she didn't disappointment me. She told me how proud she was of me and Gary, advised me not to let mess come between us and not to let our friends tell us how to handle ourselves. She told me we need to really get to know each other and build a solid foundation so that the years to come good things can be built upon it and around it, and nothing could ever shake it. When she was through, we shared a hug and a kiss, and I went to sleep, thinking how I would miss my parents, my room, and all that I had shared with them in our home.

I fell asleep but found myself wide-awake at five-thirty in the morning. I wasn't ready to get up, but after tossing and turning, I decided get up and treat myself to a long, hot bath filled with strawberry scented bubbles. As I drifted off in a deep sleep, I heard a knock at the door.

"Hey, did you fall in? I've got to get in there!" my father's voice boomed through the closed door.

I must have been asleep for a while because the bubbles were almost all gone, the water was chilly and my fingers and toes were wrinkled and cold. I quickly dried myself, put on my bathrobe and returned to my room to begin getting ready. But that's when everything started to go completely wrong!

I couldn't find my garter belt, and all the things I thought I'd put out in advance to make getting dressed go smoothly seemed far out of reach. My mother came in after her shower to help me get it all together. Then to top it all off, Lisa ran late and just made it to the church minutes before the wedding party procession started. By that time I was fine with everything, and I assured Lisa that it was okay.

It was as if Lisa's arrival put the wedding in motion. The bridal party, the young ladies dressed in satin teal blue dresses with the back out, thin lines of the fabric crisscrossed over their backs with matching sling back shoes, took their places outside of the doors of the sanctuary. They joined arms with their escorts, the men wearing black tuxes with teal blue cumber bunds and bow ties, and proceeded down the aisle as rehearsed. When I heard the music fade away until it stopped, a new flutter began in my heart as I took my father's arm and we took our places behind the sanctuary doors.

Just as the organist hit the first note of the traditional wedding march song, bubbles started floating quickly in the space where we stood, then into the sanctuary after the double doors were opened. Holding tightly to my father's arm, we walked into the church. It was standing room only. Everyone stood and several people were oohing and ahing as we started slowly down the aisle. The walk down the aisle felt like it would never end. I was glad when we reached the front. It felt like I had walked two miles!

"Who gives this bride in marriage?" asked Pastor Jackson.

"I do," my father responded, kissed my cheek and took his seat beside my mother.

Nervous tears began to fall down my cheeks and Gary put his hand under the veil to wipe them, instinctively knowing they were there. After repeating our vows before the church, Gary and I knelt, holding hands as Pastor Jackson prayed for us. At the end of the prayer, we both stood, still holding hands as our pastor said, "By the power invested in me by the Holy Spirit and the state of New Jersey, I now pronounce you husband and wife. You may salute your bride."

Lisa pulled my veil back and Gary hugged me and kissed me. We were married! We turned to greet the congregation. As they entered the church, each guest had been given a small bottle of bubbles decorated with teal and off-white flowers. As the whole wedding party proceeded down the aisle, we were greeted with bubbles, cheers and well wishes.

We rode through town honking the horns, stopped in the park for pictures then headed to the reception hall. Bubbles were flying all over the room, giving it a joyous effect. The hall and tables were decorated in our wedding colors of teal blue and off white. Each table setting had a champagne glass decorated with small flowers around the flute of the glass, and a disposable camera to take pictures of the guests at each table. Our wedding cake was on a table next to the bridal party table; it was a five-tier cake separated by what looked like bridges and a fountain on one side flowing with water colored teal blue. The band played gospel and old slow tunes. We did the traditional things, like the bridal bouquet toss and garter belt toss. Denise caught the bouquet, and one of Gary's cousins caught the garter belt. Everyone cheered and egged him to keep going up, but he stopped mid-way her thigh. Gary and I sliced and stuffed our faces with wedding cake, kissing with a mouthful for the camera. After eating the cake, we made our way around the room to greet our guests by the end of the evening.

I had just hugged Lisa and Sasha, and was hurrying to catch up with Gary who had already threatened to leave me when a man walked into the reception hall. He looked very much like Gary. He was dressed in a suit and didn't look out of place. When I saw Gary's face, I knew the man had to be his father. Gary just stood there looking stone-faced at the man, not saying a word. I'd never seen Gary look this way, like he would hit the man if he made the wrong move, so I hurried to his side. Gary made the introductions, told his father we were leaving then grabbed me by my arm almost pulling me towards the exit. We said nothing at first, and I dared not bring up the subject of his father. The little he shared with me back in high school couldn't compare with the anger I had seen in his face.

The hotel we chose was just two towns over. By the time we made it there, everything was back to normal, and Gary was smiling. We checked into the honeymoon suite and settled down for the night, putting our clothes in the drawers and hanging things up. I started the water running in the Jacuzzi while Gary turned on the stereo, putting in a slow jam tape, a little Luther Vandross and some old Blue Magic.

I guess I spent too much time in the bathroom getting ready because Gary came and knocked on the door.

"What are you doing in there? I thought we were going to get in the Jacuzzi?" Gary asked as I opened the door with a teal blue silky teddy on. Gary smiled and attempted to come towards me, but I dodged him and ran out into the room. He chased me around the room, caught me and hugged me. At that moment, I knew I wanted to be with this man for the rest of my life.

# Chapter Eleven

Driving along the winding roads of Pennsylvania, looking at the beauty of the rolling hills and different shades of greenery reminded me of my relationship with Gary. As beautiful as it looked on the outside, a change in season can cause the leaves to change color and eventually fall away, leaving the trees bare for everyone to see. After two years of "marital bliss," our marriage had changed. I was fully convinced we had made a drastic and hasty decision to marry.

We were on our way to the Pocono's to finally have the real honeymoon we never had. We knew if we didn't stop and reassess things in our relationship, there would no longer be a marriage.

A few weeks after our wedding, Gary and I started our search for a home. His mother recommended a friend of hers to lead us all around town to look at one condo after another. Some of the places were very nice, but the neighborhoods weren't so nice. Or the reverse would be true, or the price would be ridiculously high. After spending an entire morning looking at more condos and finding ourselves in yet another one that just didn't seem to be what we were looking for, we realized that what we wanted was a home with a yard big enough for our children to play in some day. We made arrangements to meet the realtor at his office the next day to go over listings for houses instead. It took a few months, but we bought our first home in a small suburb about twenty minutes from where we grew up. It was on a cul-de-sac surrounded by trees and with four other homes similar to ours. It was a raised ranch style house with four big bedrooms: The master bedroom covered half of the second floor and had a private bathroom, a formal and informal living room situated on each side of the house, a formal dining room right off the formal living room, an enormous eat-in kitchen, a finished basement with a laundry room and two spare rooms, one of which served as Gary's office and the other as a recreation room. We had a deck on the back and a big backyard. Decorating the house had been so much fun with my mother and Gary's mother giving me ideas, but once we were finished, I longed to have our first child. My own feelings caught me off guard because we didn't plan on having any children for at least another year.

Three months went by, and I still wasn't pregnant. The more I tried to put it out of my mind before it became an obsession, the more it just kept showing up in my face. Not a day went by, no matter where I was, that I didn't see a pregnant woman or a mother with her baby. With the start of school, the thought of having a child of my own disappeared when I walked into my classroom to meet my new first graders. I was right. It appeased me for a while and things were fine until around Thanksgiving.

My period was light, faint actually, and I started to feel a little run down. It was time for my check-up with my gynecologist, so I made an appointment for the following week.

While I waited for the doctor, I went over what the problem could be, chasing one crazy thought with another. Before I could put it all together, the doctor walked in. As much as I couldn't stand the internal exam, I liked the way Dr. Hollis went about it, telling me everything she was going to do before she did it and why. She always put me at ease by talking in order to distract me. After the exam, I met the doctor in her office to discuss her diagnosis. I held my breath until she told me what she found. The first word out of her mouth was "congratulations." I was surprised. When it finally sunk in that she had said I was pregnant, my body went limp with relief because, in my mind, I had conceived a tumor.

The doctor told me to make an appointment with the receptionist for one day next week so that we could begin prenatal care. At that time a routine ultra sound would be scheduled, and she would determine how far along I am and set a due date. I felt like I was floating when I half walked, half ran to my car. No sooner than I closed my car door, I whipped out my cell phone and punched in Gary's job number.

"Simmons, how may I help you?" Gary said into the phone.

"I think you've helped me enough already," I said seductively.

"Hey sweetheart, how did things go at the doctor?" he asked, his smile evident in his voice.

"Well, Daddy, you tell me 'cause see, in just a little while you will be helping me change diapers and make bottles...

"You're pregnant? We're going to have a baby? We're going to have a baby!" Gary cut me off.

Hanging up with Gary, I called my mother and told her the good news too. She screamed in my ear and I laughed. By the time we hung up, she was already talking about turning my old bedroom into a nursery and playroom for my baby.

I placed my cell phone in my purse and put an old Commissioned gospel tape into the tape player and sang along, "Love is the way..."

We were so excited about the news of our first child. Overnight, Gary became overprotective, not allowing me to lift anything too heavy, giving me back rubs and massaging my feet. The one thing I wouldn't let him do was cook because he can't even boil an egg! But we shared many nights cuddled up and playfully fighting over whether the baby would be a boy or a girl. I would be grateful for a healthy baby, boy or girl, and if the child looked like me. Overall Gary and I agreed that we wanted our child to inherit the best parts of us physically, emotionally and spiritually. We enjoyed listening to the baby's heartbeat, especially now that I was feeling little flutters that felt like feathers tickling my stomach.

A routine doctor visit in my second trimester came with the usual reminders of how I was supposed to eat and how much. When I saw the frown of concern on Dr. Hollis' face, I thought something was wrong. She immediately ordered an ultra sound for the following week because the baby's heartbeat sounded like a double beat. She assured me that there was nothing to worry about and that we should expect changes with each trimester.

Gary was unable to take off the day of the ultra sound, so I found myself sitting in the waiting room of the radiologist's office nervously twisting the strap on my purse. When the receptionist called my name, I jumped to my feet and followed the nurse to a changing room. I undressed and put on the hospital gown then waited for the technician. It was freezing cold in there too, so I rubbed my arms in an attempt to feel warm.

When the technician walked into the room, she started talking right away, introducing herself and telling me how long she worked there and how much she enjoyed her job. The technician chattered away while preparing the machine for the ultra sound. "I'm going to put some warm gel on your tummy, ok? Then we're going to watch the screen so we can see how your baby is doing."

I didn't talk much because the fact that we needed to see how my baby was doing made me a little fearful. I didn't watch the screen and felt like hopping off of that table, preferring to wait and see how my baby came out when he or she was born. That is until the technician told me to look at the screen so I could see the feet, the arms and the heads. My fear was replaced by disbelief and relief. I tried to calm myself with my own words. I couldn't contain my excitement. She couldn't give me anymore information than that, but just knowing I was having two babies had me floating all the way back home that afternoon.

Instead of calling Gary to tell him the news, I waited for him to come home that evening. As we lay in bed that night, Gary rubbed my stomach and talked to the babies. He quoted two verses of scripture to them; Psalm 127:3 and Proverbs 22:6. Gary continued to rub my stomach as he snuggled up against me until he fell asleep.

• • •

Though I decided I would work up until it was time to deliver the babies, my pregnancy went very, very well. I didn't have a day of morning sickness, but my feet swelled and I had to watch the salt in my diet. Most nights I was tired from tending to the needs of six year olds, ABC's and first grade math. It was getting harder to get around by that time, but my students often made my days, particularly when they asked to feel my stomach.

The morning of March twenty-seventh was different from any morning of my pregnancy. When I woke up, I had a dull, nagging pain in my back, but I ignored it and got up to take my shower anyway. I reasoned with myself that it was just the weight of the babies. The pain in my back stayed with me all day. Though the pain's intensity never changed, I found it necessary to stay seated behind my desk as much as possible. When my mother came to pick me up, I could hardly walk to her car. She had started picking me up when it became difficult to get behind the wheel of my car. Gary drove me to work and she picked me up. But that afternoon, I could barely get into the car, so she had to get out and help me get in. I pulled my shoes off as soon as she closed the door.

"Mom, I want to go to your house today and wait for Gary there," I said with my eyes closed.

"Are you sure you're okay?" my mother asked, putting the back of her hand on my forehead.

"Just tired, Mom."

My mother had to help me inside once we got to her house. She brought a blanket and a pillow to the den. I rested on the sofa and fell into a fitful sleep because I couldn't really get comfortable. About two hours later I woke up to the sound of Gary's voice and the feel of his kisses on my cheek.

"How are you feeling?"

"Achy and I have to use the bathroom. Help me get up." I struggled to my feet.

After using the bathroom, I realized I had blood in my underwear and checked to be sure that I was looking at blood. It was definitely blood. I started screaming for my mother. She explained that it was a sign I was about ready to give birth. I wasn't having any pain, just a lot of discomfort. By this time Gary had come upstairs to the bathroom too.

"You alright, Tonya?" he asked, looking at me and my mother and back to me again.

"Just a little spotting, Gary. I'm ready to go home," I answered, trying to hide my fear.

Then all of a sudden I was wetting myself only I had no control over it. I began to shake from fear and embarrassment. My mother grabbed several towels from the linen closet and Gary ran downstairs to get the mop. I just stood there scared to move thinking that something might happen to the babies if I did.

With my mother's help, Gary put me in the car and it didn't take long to get to the hospital. Thankfully I was pre-registered, so all we had to do was go straight up to the labor room. By this time the pain in my back was becoming excruciating and I couldn't fight the urges I had to scream at the top of my lungs. Gary could do nothing but hold my hand and sweat like he had been in a marathon race. If I wasn't in so much pain, I would have felt sorry for him.

Removing my clothes seemed to add to my pain. My stomach hardened with each contraction, and I had to stop taking off my clothes and just ride through the pain. I squeezed Gary's hand until the pain passed. By the time Gary tied the hospital gown behind me, I was exhausted and weak, and hoping that between the pains I could fall asleep.

Once the nurses had my I.V. in and me comfortably in the bed, an intern came in to do a vaginal exam. At first I protested because he looked like a linebacker, and he was a *he*! He assured me that I would be fine and that he's just trying to see how the labor was progressing. The doctor said I had dilated very fast and asked a few more questions, waiting for my responses in between contractions, assuring me that it wouldn't be long before I gave birth, and that Dr. Hollis had been informed about my progress. Then he left me alone with my pain, making me wish there was something they could do to speed up the birthing process. In the meantime I tried to relax, but the pains just seemed to get worse. Gary's presence was no longer a comfort to me. I wanted to scream, kick, holler, bite, scratch, anything to make the pain stop. Gary did all he could to comfort me, but had sense enough to leave me alone when the contractions hit me. He paced back and forth and watched me from a distance.

Dr. Hollis arrived, came into the room for a brief moment then left.

Just when I thought I could take no more, I felt a release in my body and then some pressure from between my legs. This was my first time giving birth, but I knew my babies were ready to be born.

"It's coming! It's coming!" I screamed.

Gary called a nurse. She summoned Dr. Hollis. We were ready for the delivery room. Gary followed alongside my bed as we hurried down the hallway. I don't know if it was his way of keeping up with the fast moving gurney or to give me comfort, but Gary grabbed my hand.

"I'm scared, Gary."

"It's okay, Tonya."

"Okay, but..." another pain coursed through my body, cutting off my words.

Gary played his part well, helping the nurses encourage me as I pushed the way Dr. Hollis told me. Gary was wiping sweat from my forehead when all of the pushing finally paid off. I bore down once more, and the first twin was born. Immediately he started crying loudly. My first thought was "he sure has a big mouth!"

Before I could take a deep breath, I felt the head of the second baby pushing his way out. It felt like the baby was trying to pull out all of my insides. I took a deep breath. As soon as I did, I started crying and trembling. I didn't know why because I was so happy, but the emotion I was feeling was raw and indescribable.

The nurse recorded the time of birth for both babies. Holding a clipboard in her hand, she said, "The first baby boy was born at seven p.m. weighing in at five pounds, five ounces. The second baby boy was born at seven-o-five p.m. weighing in at five pounds even."

Holding me in his arms, Gary whispered, "We have our boys, baby, we have our boys..."

After I held both of my boys, the nurses helped me get cleaned up. If I didn't know any better, I would say that Gary had those boys since they look so much like him. They were not identical. Before I was taken to the recovery room, Gary reminded me of the names we had chosen for our boys: Gary, Jr. and Gerald.

The nurse ignored my protest saying that I would be taken to recovery. In my mind I felt refreshed and my body felt like it belonged to me again. I was wide awake and feeling like somebody pumped me full of adrenaline, so I was sure I was not going to need the rest until I found myself waking up four hours later.

# Chapter Twelve

Besides the day I got married, giving birth to my sons was the happiest day of my life. Getting into a good routine with the boys was pretty rough at first, but they finally got into the swing of things. No, I think they finally got me into the swing of things. Like clockwork, after Gary Jr. is fed, Gerald wakes right up. I will probably wait at least five years to have another baby, just in case this twin thing struck me again.

It was a difficult choice but I went back to work full-time a few months after giving birth. It was hard working full-time, being a new mom and making marriage work. During the day, my mother kept the boys for me, but I had to prepare their bottles and change of clothing the evening before to cut down on what I had to do in the mornings. At the end of a typical day, I finished at school, rushed over to my mother's to get the boys and then headed home to begin dinner and get my family ready for bed. I always felt like I was packing to go on a vacation, only one never came.

By the time the boys were a year old, I had this juggling act pretty much under control, or at least that's what I wanted to believe. After another hard workday, with my arms loaded down with my brief case and with two little boys trying to run on wobbly legs, just as I closed the my car door, my cell phone rang. Somehow I managed to get it from my purse without dropping anything. Looking at the Caller ID, I saw it was Lisa calling from California. I was relieved it wasn't Gary. After a day of children and a bathroom accident one of my students had, all I wanted was some peace.

"Hey! What's up?"

"Hey, Tonya! I wanted you to be the first to hear the news. I'm getting married! I finally decided to say 'yes'!" Lisa sounded like she was about to burst, but I couldn't understand why she was so excited since she's lived with her boyfriend since she graduated from college.

"That's good, Lisa…congratulations…" I said, not being able to match my friend's excitement.

"What's wrong, Tonya? I thought you would be happy about my news."

"I am, but why did you decide to do it now? I mean marriage just isn't all it's cracked up to be…"

"I'm fully aware of that. I've never lived by the little fairy tales we grew up on. Happily ever after, my foot! I have sense enough to know that anything can touch off a problem in a relationship. Something as simple as not putting the toilet seat down, you know?" Lisa laughed but I couldn't muster up a chuckle. "Are things that bad with you and Gary?"

"Bad enough to make me have second thoughts about marrying him. Lisa, things have gotten to the point that we don't sleep in the same bed, and I'm not in any hurry to try and make things better. He just gets on my nerves with his bad attitude," I explained, tears welling up in my eyes.

Lisa said she would give me fifteen minutes to get in the house and settle in then she would call back on the house phone. When she did, I launched into the problems in my marriage. I explained that by the time the boys were eight months old, we had gotten into a real rut. Everything was about the babies for me, no romance, no time alone with my husband at all. It didn't stop Gary from trying every now and then, but I would always put him off. Since I no longer felt attractive because I still had the baby fat I gained during my pregnancy, I would block any of

Gary's attempts at romance. His kisses that were meant for my lips were purposely diverted so they could land on my cheek while I was rushing off to care for the babies. The babies had become my whole world, and Gary just existed. Along with teaching, I had no time for Gary and I reasoned something had to go lacking. For some reason, I felt Gary would understand since they were his children too. In my heart I knew I was wrong, only I didn't know what to do about it.

For the boys' first birthday, we invited family and friends and hosted the year's first cookout. We waited a few weeks into April for warmer weather. I ran around that whole day trying to get things together. My mother was my only help because Gary had disappeared and stayed away the whole day, returning just in time to see the boys cut their cake. I was embarrassed and angry with Gary, but I pretended all was well in front of our guests. The only one who wasn't fooled was my mother. She suggested we make time for each other. I explained we would get to do that once the boys were older and claimed our problems were because of Gary's inconsiderate attitude. In reality it was mine. I decided to deal with it as soon as I put the boys to bed that night.

When I confronted Gary, he just said he was here when it was important for him to be here. I felt the heat of my anger rise up the back of my neck and I stood in front of him so he could hear every word I had to say. I couldn't believe he blew off the boys' first birthday party. To add insult to injury, I told him he was treating our boys like his father had treated him all these years: abandoned them. I knew when the words left my mouth I was wrong, but I wanted Gary to hurt as much as he was hurting me. I stood my ground as he flung insulting words at me in retaliation. After we ended our argument, I went to the guestroom to sleep and ended up spending every night there for a whole month, crying myself to sleep each night.

Lisa never interrupted me as I poured out my heart to her, sharing what I felt was the worst marriage ever. When I finished, Lisa was quiet at first, giving me a chance to stop sniffing, then she let me have it. She said I was a very selfish person and couldn't see past my own feelings to see what Gary was going through. I started to correct her but she wouldn't let me get a word in. Lisa told me that I went into my marriage with my eyes open, ready to receive everything Gary had to offer me, but when he needed me, I turned my back on him. I cut him off emotionally and physically and expected him to *understand*. "If the situation were reversed, how would you feel? Where is the love of God in your heart you are always talking about, Tonya? You don't have any for your husband? What were you expecting when you married Gary? You had better make things right with your husband because nobody loves you like he does... but then you won't know that until he leaves you."

I couldn't believe my best friend was talking to me like that! I was angrier with Lisa than I had ever been with Gary. How dare she take his side after I told her everything that was going on with us? "I know I would be more understanding than Gary's been." That was all I could say because I didn't have the nerve to tell Lisa exactly how I felt. I wanted to tell her to keep her advice to herself when all she's ever known about men was to sleep with them and move on.

"Yeah right, Tonya, that's what your mouth says, but you know it's not true. Any committed relationship is more than just take; you got to give equally."

"Thanks for the advice, Lisa," I said, unable to hide the anger in my voice. "I thought you would at least listen to me and..."

"And tell you the truth. Call me when you're not mad anymore." Lisa ended the call before I could hang up.

• • •

Spending the nights alone was working my nerves, so after I thought long and hard about Lisa's advice for a few days, I made up with Gary. I apologized, but he never apologized for his actions. I guess Gary sensed that my apology wasn't really genuine because it wasn't. Our relationship stayed strained even after we both agreed we would start over again. Gary would come in from work, I would speak to him, and his answer would be "hey" with no hugs or kisses. Most times he'd leave the dinner table with his food half eaten. His attitude towards me had not changed, and his smiles and conversation was with the boys even though they could not say enough words to really talk to him. I really started to wonder why I had rushed into marriage and having children. I should have thought it through a little more before making vows that were supposed to last a lifetime. I said nothing to try and change things, but I prayed in my heart all the time for things to turn around for us.

A few weeks after we called the truce, his mother had come by to see us, but really Gary. Since he wasn't home, she sat in a chair across from me trying to wait. It became uncomfortable for us to be sitting there with nothing to talk about. Mrs. Simmons seemed a little embarrassed. She kept looking down at her hands and avoided my eyes as she talked in detail about Gary's relationship with his father. She confirmed what Gary shared with me when we were in high school. His parents could not make their marriage work, so Gary's father left and soon found happiness with another woman. After they married, Gary's stepmother did not want Gary in their lives and his father agreed with her wishes, cutting off regular communication with his son. Gary was driven by his father's actions so he tried to be the best father he knew how to be. It sort of explained why he spoiled the boys by buying them everything he could think of, even things they wouldn't be able to play with for years. He would go into their bedroom and wrestle on the floor with them, tickling them, reading to them and watching them sleep. The love for his sons was ten times more than his father had ever given to him.

Mrs. Simmons said that after ten years and his wife's death, Gary's father wanted to reconcile. Now that he was dying from cirrhosis of the liver, he was in a rush to make peace with Gary. Since the wedding, I had been hinting to Gary that he had to find a way to forgive his father. When Gary came in and his mother told him about his father's request, Gary still wasn't willing to see him. He acted like a big baby, catching an attitude and making it clear he didn't want to see his father. But to my surprise, a few days later Gary did go to see his father and it obviously brought up some emotions he had not dealt with for a while. This became another issue we had to deal with in our marriage.

When Gary went to see his father for the first time, he stayed out late and never bothered to call to let me know anything. I was angry when he came in that night and my plan was to just ignore him, but when Gary sat down at the foot of our bed and began to cry, I couldn't help but to console him and push our problems to the backburner. He told me that he tried hard to stay angry with his father and had planned to tell him how he felt about their relationship. But after seeing him, he could not do it. He just had to let go of the hurt and resentment and get to know his father again. It was painful for him to try to reach out to a dying father who was never there for him.

We then made plans to visit with Gary's father the next day. I had not seen him since the night of our wedding, but it was evident he was on his deathbed. There was an indescribable, unbearable stench coming from Mr. Simmons. He spoke in a voice so low, we had to lean close to hear him speak. From time to time his eyes would roll back in his head, then his whole body would jerk. He was barely able to gather enough strength to talk. The sunlight bothered him, so even though it was a beautiful, sunny day, he had his curtains drawn. The hiss and clicks from the I.V. machine seemed to tick in time with my own heartbeat. Gary still looked very much like him. He repeatedly apologized to Gary for leaving him and breaking up their family, asking him to be sure to take care of us and not make the same mistakes he made.

We left the hospital that day in a somber mood, barely talking because somehow we sensed Gary's father would soon die. Even the children were quiet.

The next two weeks, every night after work, Gary went to the hospital to see his father. Those nights I didn't see Gary until nine o'clock. The boys would be asleep and I would be in bed so I could wake up on time for work. He would come home with his tie loose or off and his suit jacket hanging over his shoulder and sit in the chair in our bedroom staring at nothing. We had started sleeping together again after we made up, but most nights, after visiting his father, Gary pulled a blanket out of the closet and slept in the chair. I tried to be patient and understanding, but I was beginning to feel neglected because Gary refused any of my efforts to comfort him.

One night he didn't come home at all. I woke up several times during the night to check the time only to find myself getting more and more worried. I decided that I would call his mother in the morning.

"Is Gary at your house, Mrs. Simmons?" I asked, hardly giving her a chance to say "hello."

"No, Tonya, he's probably riding around somewhere. You know his father died last night."

"No, I didn't know. He hasn't been here and he didn't call."

"Gary is angry, Tonya. First he held onto his anger against his father for all these years for leaving him, now he's angry that he didn't get a chance to know him before he left him for good. He has a lot to deal with now and I hope you're going to be as understanding as possible with him."

"Mrs. Simmons, understanding is one thing, but Gary could have at least called to tell me about his father. Through this whole thing he hasn't said a word and I've given him his space."

I listened to her a little longer then hung up. It was the weekend so I didn't have to rush out for work. In an effort not to worry about Gary so much, I placed all of my attention on the boys. I fixed the boys their breakfast. Just as we settled down in front of the T.V. to watch a "David and Goliath" religious cartoon tape, I heard the key in the door.

"Are you okay?" I asked Gary as soon as he walked in.

"Yeah..." Gary said and went upstairs to our room. I followed.

"Baby, do you want me to do anything?"

"No, Tonya...there's nothing left to do."

"What about the arrangements?" I wondered.

"My mother is going to help me with them. The woman he was with left him straight. Everything will be paid for. He even left me some money that I'll probably put into a trust fund for the boys," Gary sounded exhausted.

"You sure you don't want me to do anything for you?"

"I just want to take a hot bath and try to get some sleep. I have to go to the funeral home with my mother this afternoon."

I ran some water and placed two vanilla-scented candles by the sink. I closed the blind and turned the light off before I let Gary know his bath was ready. He came in and sank down in the water, flinching a little because it was hot. I began taking his cloth and squeezing water down his back and massaging his neck, kissing his ears and chest. It's been about seven or eight months since we'd made love, and it didn't take long for my dormant desires to come to the surface. Then Gary stopped me.

"Not now, okay? Why don't you let me take my bath by myself?"

"I was trying to make you feel better..."

"Not now...maybe later..."

I walked out of the bathroom and slammed the door. My eyes burned from the tears I was holding back. I decided then that Gary and I both needed some time alone, so I left him at home and went to visit my mother. After taking the boys to the den to play with their toys, I returned to the kitchen to talk to my mother. She could tell something was wrong, so she sat down in a chair across from me at the kitchen table and said, "What's going on with you and Gary?"

"We haven't made any progress, his father died last night and I'm thinking about giving him the space he needs," I said folding my arms across my chest waiting to hear her motherly advice.

"Your husband needs you," was all she said. She then got up from her chair to stir a pot on the stove. Without even looking at me, she told me to leave the boys with her so I could help Gary get through this time. I started to plead my case, but she wouldn't hear it and sent me on my way.

As I drove back to my house, I called Lisa on my cell phone to tell her that Gary lost his father. I only called her, hoping to get a different opinion, and use the situation as an excuse to talk to her again. We hadn't spoken since she sided with Gary when I told her about the problems in my marriage. She told me she learned in her relationship with her fiancé that for all that she was taking from him, she should have been giving... of her time, a listening ear, a hug, a kind word, whatever it took to make him feel loved. She told me to do the same and really think things over, especially at this time because Gary really needed me. Hanging up, I realized Lisa had really matured. She had learned to take responsibility for the things she had done.

When I pulled up in front of my house, Gary and his mother were coming out of the house to head for the funeral home to make the arrangements. At first I wasn't going to go, but my mother's words echoed in my head, reminding me to be there for my husband. Struggling with my emotions so I would not act the way I honestly felt, I offered to go with them to the funeral home. Without even looking at me, Gary said, "Yeah...come on" in a flat emotionless voice. Gary rode up front with his mother, and I sat in the back.

We arrived at the funeral home, and followed closely behind Gary's mother. A bell went off when we opened the door. A man greeted us. He spoke using a soothing tone, asking us to come to his office to discuss their services and prices before we view the body. I had no intentions of viewing the body, but Gary and his mother went with the funeral director to view it. Gary came back to the office within five minutes after going to see his father, hardly able to compose himself as he went through a series of emotions. He was angry and hurt. When I reached out to take his hand, he pulled it away, so I got up to look out of the window until Mrs. Simmons returned with the funeral director. The funeral director was nice and sympathetic. He had this weird look, like he was wearing the makeup he used for the dead people. He spoke in a monotone voice and talked about death and the preparations as if he were going to decorate our home.

Unfortunately, nothing the funeral director said consoled Gary. He refused to discuss the service for his father, and sat off to the side with me while he let his mother choose the casket and other arrangements needed to schedule the funeral. We had so many choices and it was downright expensive! Not that I really knew how much funerals were, but six or seven thousand dollars was more than I ever expected.

Mrs. Simmons' hands were shaking when she signed the papers. She asked Gary if he would like to look over the paper work before they left, but he shook his head and got up from his chair, stuffing his hands in his pockets, sniffling while he tried to keep his tears from falling.

The funeral service set for the following Tuesday. We rode back to our house in total silence. Gary's mother decided to come inside to visit a while. She and I took a seat in the informal living room while we waited for Gary to join us.

While Gary busied himself in the kitchen, Mrs. Simmons started talking to me about Gary and how she wished we could work out our differences. I told her I would certainly try my best. She stayed a little longer to finalize plans with Gary so that we knew what had to be done before the funeral. I was glad when she decided it was time for her to leave so we could stop talking about death, the funeral and anything else associated with it. When Gary came back in the house after walking his mother to her car, he brought in the toys the boys had left on the front lawn. I was headed up the stairs to finish my housecleaning when Gary called me back to the living room to start an argument! That had to be his intentions because he asked me did I want our marriage to work. We volleyed questions back at each other, each refusing to commit to anything.

Gary asked, "Do you think we should agree to part until we can get ourselves together?"

This was like a slap in the face and instantly brought tears to my eyes.

"You...you really think that...separating is going to make things better? You honestly believe that?" I was dumbfounded.

"I don't know..."

"I started to leave this morning, I really did..."

"I knew you did, that's why I'm openly giving you that option..."

"You're not giving me anything! And you know what else? I'm tired of trying when you don't!"

"Girl, please! You won't let me touch you for months, then all of sudden you gonna push up on me when I'm grieving. What's that? I'm not that vulnerable!"

"You're the one who had to have kids! Now you got them and I have to take care of them, with little help from you. Then you expect me to be some kind of machine and be ready to part my legs at your command. I can't do it all, Gary!" I said, feeling like I could strangle him.

"I've never expected you to be anybody but you. But who I thought you to be, you're not."

"What do you mean I'm not me? Who else could I be?"

"Some selfish woman who don't have time or love for her husband. What do you call what you did this morning? The kids were downstairs then, so why today?"

The tears I'd been fighting so hard to hold back streamed down my face, my voice cracking with the hurt I'd tried equally as hard to hide.

"For the record, I was trying to show you that I wasn't selfish and I wanted to make you feel better. You didn't bother to call me last night and tell me that your father died. I blew that off. You don't come home until this morning and I blow that off too. What happened in the bathroom wasn't something I planned. I genuinely wanted to give you my love. I haven't felt that way in a very long time, and I guess I won't have to again."

I turned and went upstairs to the kids' room to clean up their toys and make their beds. While I was putting their things away, Gary came into their room and started helping me. That was a first for him, but I didn't say anything, as we cleaned the kids' room in silence. I looked around to make sure everything was done then started to go down the hall to clean the bathroom, but Gary called me back to him. Reluctantly I went back into the boys' room and braced myself to hear what he had to say. Instead of the angry words I expected, Gary held his arms out to me and I went into his embrace, unable to fight the need to feel his arms around me. Sighing heavily, Gary held me tighter still and then whispered in my ear, "Tonya, I'm so sorry...let's talk, ok?"

Our apologies turned into touches to reassure our love for each other, those touches into caresses and soft kisses, and then soft kisses into hungry ones. We spent the rest of the day in our bedroom, making love, trying to make up for the times we didn't.

The days after the funeral were rough. At times, Gary became quiet or he would be angry and take it out on me. Through it all, I was thankful that Gary wasn't as distant as he had been. So we planned a trip, for just the two of us. We decided not to go far, just to the Poconos since we were watching our finances. I recalled the beauty of the place. As a child, I often vacationed there with my parents. Our plans were to stay for an entire week, so Gary took his time driving to our hotel destination. We stopped as often as we could just to look in stores and buy silly things along the way, igniting the love that I thought was gone from our marriage. Through our problems I learned that marriage isn't just enjoying the good times, but being able to endure through the bad times and still have the love between us intact. We held hands a lot and shared a silent peace. I treasured this moment, and hoped it would get us through the days ahead.

## Chapter Thirteen

The Poconos was the perfect choice for Gary and I to get away. I'd forgotten, in high school, Gary had been one of the biggest jokesters. It felt good to hear his jokes. The first few days we went on long walks holding hands. In that short time I had come to love my husband more, grateful for heeding Lisa's advice and accepted that the selfishness I saw in myself wasn't good for my marriage or my family.

Gary and I agreed that we would spend this time getting to know each other again and decided we wouldn't bother my mother about the boys until we were on our way back home. That way we could concentrate on the reason we decided to get away from home in the first place.

We went horseback riding the third day. By the time we were through with the horses, we were hot, sweaty and dusty. I was looking forward to a hot shower and nap once we returned to the hotel. When we entered our room, the message light on the phone was blinking. I didn't want to check the message, but there was no way I couldn't. When I heard my mother's voice, I started to tremble. She only said to call her as soon as I got back to my room. She assured me the boys were fine, but I could tell something was wrong. I steeled myself and sat down on the bed as my mother explained that she had received word that Sasha was in the hospital and she wasn't doing so well.

I cried while we packed our clothes for the return home. I prayed for Sasha, unable to bear the thought of losing her. After going through the funeral for Gary's father, I'd had enough of death and dying.

On the drive home, Gary held my hand and I laid my head on his shoulder for comfort. Thinking back on the few days we spent alone together, I was grateful for the new level we had reached in our relationship. We took time to pray, something we had gotten out of the habit of doing once the boys were born. During the three-hour drive, I had plenty of time to reflect on Sasha and the times we shared growing up. It seemed she never had a good life, but you couldn't tell because she was the most enthusiastic person I knew. She always rebounded from life's hardships, first, with her mother abusing alcohol and men, and then contracting the HIV virus. She was very afraid for a long time, but as time went on, we all pretty much accepted it and expected Sasha to live a long life. What I regretted the most was not staying in touch with her like I should have had. The last time I saw her was right after the boys were born. She came to the house with bags of gifts for them and stayed the whole day with me. We talked and laughed, catching up on what we both were doing. She still worked as a paralegal, and she and Quadir had finally gotten officially engaged and then eloped, spending a week in Vegas to honeymoon. For now, having children was out of the question. With the treatment of AIDs and the advances they were making every day, she thought maybe one day she would be able to have a child.

Every now and then Sasha and I would talk on the phone, but just to say hello and to check on each other. Long gone were the days of meeting for dinner and hanging out together. I wished I had made time. So I continued to pray that God would bring her through. This was Sasha's first hospital stay that I knew about, but that still didn't ease my fear that she would die. By the time we reached our town, I had fallen asleep. Gary woke me and asked if I would like to stop at the hospital before we went to my parent's house. I pulled the visor down in front of me to use the mirror to comb my hair and rub the sleep out of the corners of my eyes. I wasn't too sure I was ready to see Sasha.

She had lost so much weight, and her skin was so dark! Sasha's illness had marked itself all over her skin with dry, scaly legions.

"Sasha?" I whispered.

"Oh, hey, Tonya...glad you could come. I would sit up, but I have to call my body strength way ahead of time to do that," she said with a smile. "How was the Poconos? Another bun in the oven?"

"No, Sasha, but the Poconos was good. How're you feeling?" I asked, taking the subject off of me.

"Probably a heck of a lot better than I look. At least Quadir says I'm looking better every day. He lies," Sasha said, looking a little sad.

"When are you getting out of here?"

"Girl, I'm not expecting to get out of here at all. I mean, I'm trying to deal with that fact, you know? I have the full blown thing now and they've pretty much done all they're gonna do."

"Sasha, do you want to come out of here?" Gary walked to the other side of the bed. "The reason I'm asking you is so I'll know how to pray for you. If you've resigned to the fact that you won't, then it's no use in praying for that."

"I want to, really I do, but the doctors already told me I won't."

"So you accept their word as the final word?" Gary asked.

"Who else is going to change it?"

"God can change anything. If you want to go home, we'll pray that God will strengthen you and raise you up. Is that what you want?"

"Yeah...I really want to go home again."

"That's what we'll pray for."

Gary and I took Sasha's hands and my husband prayed for Sasha. I know that Sasha was strengthened as tears flowed down her face and she praised God! Sasha said that she knew she had made peace with God and that she was thankful for what He had done for her. We each hugged her and visited with Sasha for another fifteen minutes. She still had her beautiful smile and her quick, smart mouth, but she was so weak and tired. Seeing my friend like this broke my heart, and the tears that I had been keeping back broke through just as we reached our car. Gary pulled me into a hug and let me cry it all out on his chest.

I stayed in a somber mood during the week. I went through the motions of carrying out my daily responsibilities, but it was hard to smile, hard to be happy knowing that I was about to lose one of my best friends. I still didn't know how to handle it in my mind, but in my heart I believed Sasha would be better off dead than staying alive and suffering with constant pain and weakness. Yet I still held onto to the words of the prayer and continually asked God not to let my friend die.

By the end of that week, Sasha was released from the hospital and she was able to walk with the aid of a walker. It made her look like she should be a resident of a senior citizens home, but at least she was getting around a little better. The doctors said this happened sometimes, when the disease will give the patient a reprieve. But we knew God did the work. Praise Him! Sasha was full of life and strength throughout the rest of the summer. She even started attending church services so that she could keep what God had given her. But by Christmas, she had a relapse. Back in the hospital she went, with Quadir constantly by her side. When I arrived at the hospital, Sasha's mother was there. She seemed and smelled drunk.

"I know you came here to encourage her, but this is it. I dealt with this same thing with my moms," Quadir said to me when I came to visit Sasha. I believe it was more to comfort him than it was for us.

"God can do for her what He did before, Quadir. If that's what Sasha wants," I said.

"Guys look, I'm tired. I've been fighting this thing for a long time and I'm tired. Do you think God will be mad if I'm ready to go?" Sasha asked, looking deep into my eyes. "I told my mother the other day to get ready because I can't deal with the pain anymore."

"Sasha, please..." I began to protest.

"Tonya, I love you, girl. I love all of you. But enough is enough. These last few months have been the best of my whole entire life. I'm satisfied, I'm so content..."

There was nothing I could say to Sasha to change what I knew she felt. We all tried to be brave for her, but Sasha was doing a good job of being brave for us.

"Tonya, I'm glad you came..." Sasha said in a very low voice, as her eyes rolled to the back of her head.

Quadir placed his head on Sasha's chest and wept loudly, telling her he loves her and will miss her. She rubbed his head with her hand and shed some tears too. When he ceased crying he stood up and took one hand and I took the other. Sasha looked at us both and said:

"I'm first to go, but you know what? You're all JEAL...you remember that, Tonya? I love you..." she said, her voice barely audible.

Sasha smiled weakly, closed her eyes and let out her last breath. I ran out and called Gary at work and cried for fifteen minutes on the phone. I heard the doctor tell the nurses to get security to remove her mother, who was totally hysterical. Quadir just stayed there, holding her hand and crying. Unreal and yet so real...

I left the hospital with a handful of tissues headed for my parked car. I couldn't drive until I calmed myself down, so I took my cell phone out. I could hear my mother weeping softly over the phone. We cried together. Letting out all the emotions soothed me and I was able to start my car and head home.

As soon as I walked in the house, the phone was ringing. It was Lisa. My mother said she would call over to Lisa's parents' house to tell them about Sasha.

"Oh Tonya! Sasha's gone, Sasha's gone!" Lisa cried into the phone.

"I know...I was there with her..."

"You...were...there?" Lisa asked between sniffles.

"Yeah..."

"I already made plane reservations and I've got to leave before I miss my flight. I'll call you as soon as I land in New York. Could you come get me at the airport?" Lisa asked and hung up before I could answer.

I didn't know what to do with myself, so I paced from one end of the house to the other trying to find something to do to fight the urge to run. My friend was gone and there was nothing I could do about it, nothing anyone could say to make me feel better about it. Then the doorbell rang. When I opened the door, Denise stood there with tears flowing down her face and I grabbed her and we held each other tightly, crying on one another's shoulders. Once we calmed down, I invited Denise in for some tea so we could talk. We still had some unresolved issues between us. Losing Sasha so soon left me with regrets, and I didn't want to have any between Denise and me. We sat in my kitchen for the rest of the day into the early evening, sipping tea, crying and making amends for all of the past hurts and mean words we had exchanged. In spite of the common grief we shared, we also shared some happiness because of our mended friendship. I just wished we had done this before we lost Sasha.

By the time we drank our last cup of tea and Denise was ready to leave, my doorbell rang for the second time that day. When I opened the door, it was Lisa! She had cut her hair down and dyed it a light brown color, her eyebrows too. Lisa's casual black dress surprised me because the last time I saw her, she was showing everything she could without getting arrested for indecent exposure. She said she couldn't wait for someone to pick her up so she rented a car.

"Aren't you going to invite me in? It's been a long day," Lisa said, hugging me and then following me to the kitchen. She was surprised and relieved to see Denise sitting there. Denise got up to meet her hug, grabbing up a few tissues for the both of them. We sat around the kitchen table and it was almost like old times. Sasha's absence hung in the air and caused several minutes of silence between us. We were together to mourn our close friend through our tears, our memories that made us laugh and those that made us wish we could turn back the hands of time. This was the most difficult day of our lives, and losing Sasha seemed to strengthen our friendship.

## Chapter Fourteen

Sasha had already made arrangements and Quadir had to take care of most of them because Sasha's mother couldn't. Sasha, being Sasha, even had her funeral planned to the "T." She wanted me to sing "His Eye is on the Sparrow", only I wished we were doing it in four-part harmony like when we sang it that time in my room. My mother still had the tape and asked if Quadir would play it at the funeral.

The services were a one-day thing because Sasha said she would get cold showing herself for two days. I could hear her saying that as if she were talking to me right now. All of us, Lisa, Denise and myself, had a chance to talk about our friend at her funeral. It was hard, but we managed to get a few laughs knowing that Sasha would want it that way.

When I had to speak, Quadir played the tape of us singing first. I cried because I hadn't heard it since we were kids. Sasha's voice rang out loud and clear, and a whole lot of people cried. Then I was called to the podium to sing.

"I can remember the day we made this tape. It feels like it was just yesterday," I said, addressing the congregation of people. "We'd gone to the mall and Sasha was the one who suggested we sing together. I wasn't allowed to sing blues, so we decided on this song since we were doing it at my house. I thought Sasha was kidding, but as you heard, she had a nice voice. She would say this was a way to make the girls JEAL, and the guys would be sweatin' us. Sasha...my girl, my friend. We went different ways as we approached adulthood, but we have always, always remained friends. I'm going to miss you, Sasha..."

I sang like never before. The Lord anointed my voice and I hit notes that I remember I couldn't. I didn't practice the song either. When I was through, people were praising God! I praised Him too. I concluded with, "If Sasha were here, she would be saying: Girl, look at them. You know the women are JEAL, oh ye-e-e-e-eah!

• • •

At times, trying to cope with Sasha's death is a little hard on me, so I took to going to the mall or for long rides alone. I would find myself driving toward the mall on a day that I couldn't seem to pull it together. I had just listened to the tape of us singing. The very place that was an important part of our teen years had now become a place for me to walk and think. The memories that would always flood me were well worth my time.

As I walked along the halls of the mall reminiscing about my friends, I couldn't help remembering the things I'd gone through over the years. There was a time I didn't know whether I was coming or going, who I was or what I wanted to be. But I got it together, when I made a vow to God to give myself totally to Him. It wasn't an overnight thing, it has and will be a process, a lifelong one as I continue to live for God and learn His will for my life. I'd come to realize that my family life and career had to all come unto subjection to what I committed to God because they are all a certain part of me. God is first, but after Him is my husband and children who I love so much. The time I put in with the Youth Department of my church, and teaching my first grade class. These things make up the person I am, but I take all of who I am and give it all to God. He entrusted me with all these things, so for all of me,

I belong to God and He belongs to me. I am grateful every day I chose to yield my life to the calling He has for my life.

But then I have to stop and ask myself, Have I really given all of me? All of me…that's a lot to give. I understand it to be a daily process that will include some ups and downs, some happy times and some sad times, some disappointments and some accomplishments, but I'm up for the task. It is most definitely a great sacrifice, one I can never turn my back on. It is full of love, commitment, hope, joy and peace that only God can give. It is He who makes my life complete because for all of me that I give to Him in reverence for all He is to me, truly I can say that I have given all of me. Most certainly I am grateful that I have yielded to the call He has for my life.

# The End

## About The Author

Born and raised in Plainfield, New Jersey, Sharel E. Gordon-Love started writing at the age of six, winning immediate recognition for her essays and short stories. Her first nonfiction work, *"Is There Hope for the Black Male?"* was published by Black Child Magazine in 1994.

Certified in Microcomputer Technology and Business Administration, Mrs. Gordon-Love graduated from Berkeley College of Business in 1993. She is currently employed as a Quality Assurance SOP Administrator for a multi-national skin care corporation in Norwalk, CT.

A licensed evangelist, Sharel and her family attend Holy Tabernacle Church of God in Christ in Bridgeport, Connecticut. There she serves as President of the Youth Department, and is also actively involved in the Sunday School and Children's Church ministries.

Ms. Gordon-Love, resides in north Bridgeport, Connecticut with her three sons and daughter.